One More for the Road

Books by Ray Bradbury

Ahmed and the Oblivion
  Machines

Dandelion Wine

Dark Carnival

Death Is a Lonely Business

Driving Blind

Fahrenheit 451

From the Dust Returned

The Golden Apples
  of the Sun

A Graveyard for Lunatics

Green Shadows, White Whale

The Halloween Tree

I Sing the Body Electric!

The Illustrated Man

Journey to Far Metaphor

Kaleidoscope

Long After Midnight

The Martian Chronicles

The Machineries of Joy

A Medicine for Melancholy

The October Country

One More for the Road

One Timeless Spring

Quicker Than the Eye

R Is for Rocket

The Stories of Ray Bradbury

S Is for Space

Something Wicked This Way
  Comes

The Toynbee Convector

When Elephants Last in the
  Dooryard Bloomed

Witness and Celebrate

Yestermorrow

Zen in the Art of Writing

WILLIAM MORROW

AN IMPRINT OF HARPERCOLLINSPUBLISHERS

One More
for the Road

a new story collection by

RAY BRADBURY

im" in the fall 1947 issue

of *Playboy*; copyright ©

000 issue of *The Magazine of Fantasy and Science* .... .adbury.

"The Dragon Danced at Midnight" first appeared in the July 1966 issue of *Cavalier* under the title "The Year the Glop Monster Won the Golden Lion at Cannes," copyright © 1966 by Fawcett Publications; copyright renewed 1994 by Ray Bradbury.

"The Laurel and Hardy Alpha Centauri Farewell Tour" first appeared in the Spring 2000 issue of *Amazing Stories*; copyright © 2000 by Ray Bradbury.

"With Smiles as Wide as Summer" first appeared in the November 1961 issue of *Clipper*; copyright © 1961; copyright renewed 1989 by Ray Bradbury.

"The Enemy in the Wheat" first appeared in the August 1984 issue of *New Rave*; copyright © 1984 by Ray Bradbury.

"Fore!" first appeared in the October/November 2001 issue of *The Magazine of Fantasy and Science Fiction*; copyright © 2001 by Ray Bradbury.

HarperCollins books may be purchased for educational, business, or sales promotional use. For information please write: Special Markets Department, HarperCollins Publishers Inc., 10 East 53rd Street, New York, NY 10022.

FIRST EDITION

Designed by Claire Vaccaro

Printed on acid-free paper

Library of Congress Cataloging-in-Publication Data

Bradbury, Ray, 1920–
   One more for the road : a new story collection / Ray Bradbury.
      p.   cm.
   ISBN 0-06-621106-9
      I. Title.
PS3503.R167 O54 2002
813'.54—dc21   2001026384

02   03   04   05   06   RRD   10   9   8   7   6   5   4   3   2   1

To DONALD HARKINS,
dear friend, dearly remembered
with love

This book is dedicated
with love and gratitude to
FORREST J. ACKERMAN,
who took me out of high school and got me started on
my writing career way back in 1937

Contents

First Day   1

Heart Transplant   13

Quid Pro Quo   25

After the Ball   37

In Memoriam   47

Tête-à-Tête   55

The Dragon Danced at Midnight   63

The Nineteenth   81

Beasts   87

Autumn Afternoon   105

Where All Is Emptiness There Is
      Room to Move   111

One-Woman Show   129

The Laurel and Hardy Alpha Centauri
      Farewell Tour   139

Leftovers   153

One More for the Road   167

Tangerine   179

With Smiles as Wide as Summer   197

Time Intervening   203

The Enemy in the Wheat   211

Fore!   223

My Son, Max   231

The F. Scott/Tolstoy/Ahab Accumulator   241

Well, What Do You Have to Say for Yourself?   253

Diane de Forêt   261

The Cricket on the Hearth   269

Afterword: Metaphors, the Breakfast
   of Champions   285

One More
for the Road

First Day

IT WAS WHILE he was eating breakfast that Charles Douglas glanced at his newspaper and saw the date. He took another bite of toast and looked again and put the paper down.

"Oh, my God," he said.

Alice, his wife, startled, looked up. "What?"

"The date. Look at it! September fourteenth."

"So?" Alice said.

"The first day of school!"

"Say that again," she said.

"The first day of school, you know, summer vacation's over, everyone back, the old faces, the old pals."

Alice studied him carefully, for he was beginning to rise. "Explain that."

"It is the first day, isn't it," he said.

"What's that got to do with us?" she said. "We don't have family, we don't know any teachers, we don't even have friends anywhere near with kids."

"Yeah, but . . ." Charlie said, picking up the newspaper again, his voice gone strange. "I promised."

"Promised? Who?"

"The old gang," he said. "Years ago. What time is it?"

"Seven-thirty."

"We'd better hurry then," he said, "or we'll miss it."

"I'll get you more coffee. Take it easy. My God, you look terrible."

"But I just remembered." He watched her pour his cup full. "I promised. Ross Simpson, Jack Smith, Gordon Haines. We took almost a blood oath. Said we'd meet again, the first day of school, fifty years after graduation."

His wife sat back and let go of the coffeepot.

"This all has to do with the first day of school, 1938?"

"Yeah, '38."

"And you stood around with Ross and Jack and what's his—"

"Gordon! And we didn't just stand around. We knew we were going out in the world and might not meet again for years, or never, but we took a solemn oath, no matter what, we'd all remember and come back, across the world if we had to, to meet out in front of the school by the flagpole, 1988."

"You all promised that?"

"Solemn promise, yeah. And here I am sitting here talking when I should be getting the hell out the door."

"Charlie," Alice said, "you realize that your old school is forty miles away."

"Thirty."

"Thirty. And you're going to drive over there and—"

"Get there before noon, sure."

"Do you know how this sounds, Charlie?"

"Nuts," he said, slowly. "Go ahead, say it."

"And what if you get there and nobody else shows?"

"What do you mean?" he said, his voice rising.

"I mean what if you're the only damn fool who's crazy enough to believe—"

He cut in. "They promised!"

"But that was a lifetime ago!"

"They promised!"

"What if in the meantime they changed their minds, or just forgot?"

"They wouldn't forget."

"Why not?"

"Because they were my best pals, best friends forever, no one ever had friends like that."

"Ohmigod," she said. "You're so sad, so naive."

"Is that what I am? Look, if I remember, why not them?"

"Because you're a special loony case!"

"Thanks a lot."

"Well, it's true, isn't it? Look at your office upstairs, all those Lionel trains, Mr. Machines, stuffed toys, movie posters."

"And?"

"Look at your files, full of letters from 1960, 1950, 1940, you can't throw away."

"They're special."

"To you, yes. But do you really think those friends, or strangers, have saved your letters, the way you've saved theirs?"

"I write great letters."

"Darn right. But call up some of those correspondents, ask for some of your old letters back. How many do you think will return?"

He was silent.

"Zilch," she said.

"No use using language like that," he said.

"Is 'zilch' a swearword?"

"The way you say it, yes."

"Charlie!"

"Don't 'Charlie' me!"

"How about the thirtieth anniversary of your drama club group where you ran hoping to see some bubblehead Sally or something or other, and she didn't remember, didn't know who you were?"

"Keep it up, keep it up," he said.

"Oh, God," she said. "I don't mean to rain on your picnic, I just don't want you to get hurt."

"I've got a thick skin."

"Yes? You talk bull elephants and go hunt dragonflies."

He was on his feet. With each of her comments he got taller.

"Here goes the great hunter," he said.

"Yes," she exhaled, exhausted. "There you go, Charlie."

"I'm at the door," he said.

She stared at him.

"I'm gone."

And the door shut.

MY GOD, he thought, this is like New Year's Eve.

He hit the gas hard, then released it, and hit it again, and let it slow, depending on the beehive filling his head.

Or it's like Halloween, late, the fun over, and everyone going home, he thought. Which?

So he moved along at an even pace, constantly glancing at his watch. There was enough time, sure, plenty of time, but he had to be there by noon.

But what in hell is this? he wondered. Was Alice right? A chase for the wild goose, a trip to nowhere for nothing? Why was it so damned important? After all, who were those pals, now unknown, and what had they been up to? No letters, no phone calls, no face-to-face collisions by pure accident, no obituaries. That last, scratch that! Hit the accelerator, lighten up! Lord, he thought, I can hardly wait. He laughed out loud. When was the last time you said that? When you were a kid, could hardly wait, had a list of hard-to-wait-for things. Christmas, my God, was always a billion miles off. Easter? Half a million. Halloween? Dear sweet Halloween, pumpkins, running, yelling, rapping windows, ringing doorbells, and the mask, cardboard smelling hot with breath over your face. All Hallows! The best. But a lifetime away. And July Fourth with great expectations, trying to be first out of bed, first half-dressed, first jumping out on the lawn, first to light six-inchers, first to blow up the town! Hey, listen! First! July Fourth. Can hardly wait. Hardly wait!

But, back then, almost every day was can-hardly-wait day. Birthdays, trips to the cool lake on hot noons, Lon Chaney films, the Hunchback, the Phantom. Can hardly wait. Digging ravine caves. Magicians arriving in the long years. Can't wait. Hop to it. Light the sparklers. Won't wait. Won't.

He let the car slow, staring ahead across Time.

Not far now, not long. Old Ross. Dear Jack. Special Gordon. The gang. The invincibles. Not three but four, counting himself, Musketeers.

He ran the list, and what a list. Ross, the handsome dog, older than the rest though they were all the same age, bright but no show-off, bicycling through classes with no sweat, getting high marks with no care. Reader of books, lover of Fred Allen Wednesdays radio, repeater of all the best jokes next day noon. Meticulous dresser, though poor. One good tie, one good belt, one coat, one pair of pants, always pressed, always clean. Ross. Yeah, sure, Ross.

And Jack, the future writer who was going to conquer the world and be the greatest in history. So he yelled, so he said, with six pens in his jacket and a yellow pad waiting to un-Steinbeck Steinbeck. Jack.

And Gordon, who loped across campus on the bodies of

moaning girls, for all he had to do was glance and the females were chopped like trees.

Ross, Jack, Gordon, what a team.

Fast and slow he drove, now slow.

But what will they think of me? Have I done enough, have I done too well? Ninety stories, six novels, one film, five plays—not bad. Hell, he thought, I won't say, who cares, just shut your mouth, let them talk, you listen, the talk will be great.

What do we say first, I mean as soon as we show up, the old gang, by the flagpole? Hello? Hi. My God, you're really here! How you been, what's new, you okay, good health? Marriage, children, grandchildren, pictures, 'fess up. What, what?

Okay, he thought, you're the writer. Make something up, not just hi, a celebration. Write a poem. Good grief, would they stand still for a poem? How about, would it be too much: I love you, love you all. No. Above and beyond. I love you.

He slowed the car even more, looking through the windshield at shadows.

But what if they don't show? They will. They must. And if they show, everything will be all right, won't it? Boys being what they are, if they've had a bad life, bad marriages, you name it, they won't show. But if it's been good, absolutely incredibly good, they'll show. That'll be the proof, won't it? They've done well so it's okay to remember the date and arrive. True or false? True!

He stepped on the gas, sure that they'd all be there. Then he slowed again, sure that they wouldn't. Then stepped on the gas again. What the hell, by God, what the hell.

And he pulled up in front of the school. Beyond belief, there was a place to park, and not many students by the flagpole, a handful at most. He wished there were more, to camouflage the arrival of his friends; they wouldn't want to arrive and be seen right off, would they? He wouldn't. A slow progression through the noon crowd and then the grand surprise, wouldn't that be the ticket?

He hesitated getting out of the car until a small crowd emerged from the school, young men and women, all talking at once and pausing by the flagpole, which made him happy, for now there were enough to hide latecomers, no matter what age. He got out of the car and at first did not turn, afraid to look, afraid maybe there'd be no one there, no one would come, no one would have remembered, the whole thing was dumb. He resisted the temptation to jump back in the car and go away.

The flagpole was deserted. There were a lot of students around it, nearby, but nobody right at the flagpole.

He stood staring at it as if by staring someone would move up, go by, perhaps touch it.

His heart slowed, he blinked, and started instinctively to leave.

When, from the edge of the crowd, a man moved.

An old man, hair white, step slow, face pale. An old man.

And then two more old men.

Oh Lord, he thought, is that them? Did they remember? What's next?

They stood in a wide circle, not speaking, hardly looking, making no move, for the longest time.

Ross, he thought, is that you? And the next one: Jack, now, yes? And the final one. Gordon?

Their expressions were all the same. The same thoughts must have been moving behind each face.

Charlie leaned forward. The others leaned forward. Charlie took the smallest step. The three others took the smallest step. Charlie glanced over at each face. They did the same, trading glances. And then—

Charlie stepped back. After a long moment the other men stepped back. Charlie waited. The three old men waited. The flag blew, softly flapping, on the high pole.

A bell rang somewhere inside the school. Lunchtime over. Time to go in. The students dispersed across the campus.

With the students moving away, with the crowd leaving so there was no camouflage, no more cover, the four men stood in a great circle around the flagpole, some fifty or sixty feet separating them, the four points of a bright autumn day compass.

Perhaps one of them wet his lips, perhaps one of them blinked, perhaps one of them shuffled one shoe forward, took it back. The white hair on their heads blew in the wind. A wind took up the flag on the pole and blew it straight out. Inside the school, another bell rang, with finality.

He felt his mouth shape words but say nothing. He repeated the names, the wondrous names, the loving names, in whispers only he could hear.

He did not make a decision. His lower body did it in a half turn, his legs followed, as did his feet. He stepped back and stood sideways.

Across a great distance, one by one in the blowing noon wind, first one stranger and then the next followed by the next half-turned, stepped a half step away, and waited.

He felt his body hesitate and want to move forward and not off toward his car. Again, he made no decision. His shoes, disembodied, took him quietly away.

As did the bodies, the feet, and the shoes of the strangers.

Now he was on the move, now they were on the move, all walking in different directions, slowly, half-glancing back at the deserted flagpole and the flag, abandoned, high, flapping quietly, and the lawn in front of the school empty and inside the moment of loud talk and laughter and the shove of chairs being put in place.

They were all in motion now, half-glancing back at the empty flagpole.

He halted for a moment, unable to move his feet. He gazed back a final time with a tingling in his right hand, as if it wanted to rise. He half-lifted and looked at it.

And then, across sixty or seventy yards of space, beyond the flagpole, one of the strangers, only half-looking, raised his hand and waved it quietly, once, on the silent air. Over to one side, another old man, seeing this, did the same, as did the third.

He watched as his hand and arm slowly lifted and the tips of his fingers, up in the air, gestured the least small gesture. He looked up at his hand and over at the old men.

My God, he thought, I was wrong. Not the first day of school. The last.

.   .   .

ALICE HAD SOMETHING frying in the kitchen that smelled good.

He stood in the doorway for a long moment.

"Hey," she said, "come in, take a load off your feet."

"Sure," he said, and went to the dining-room table and saw that it was laid out with the best silver and the best dinnerware and candles lit that were usually lit for a twilight meal, and the best napkins in place, while Alice waited in the kitchen door.

"How did you know I'd be here so soon?" he said.

"I didn't," she said. "I saw you pull up out front. Bacon and eggs are quick, be ready in a sec. Sit down?"

"That's an idea." He held to the back of one chair and studied the cutlery. "Sit down."

He sat and she came and kissed him on the brow and went back to the kitchen.

"Well?" she called.

"Well, what?"

"How did it go?" she called.

"How did what go?"

"You know," she said. "The big day. All those promises. Did anyone show?"

"Sure," he said. "Everyone showed," he added.

"Well, spill the beans."

She was in the kitchen doorway now, bringing the bacon and eggs. She studied him.

"You were saying?"

"Was I?" He leaned forward over the table. "Oh, yeah."

"Well, was there lots to talk about?"

"We—"

"Yes?"

He saw the waiting and empty plate.

And tears falling on the plate.

"God, yes!" he said, very loud. "We talked our heads off!"

Heart
Transplant

"WOULD I WHAT?" he asked, in the dark, lying there easily, looking at the ceiling.

"You heard me," she said, lying there beside him with similar ease, holding his hand, but staring rather than looking at that ceiling, as if there were something there that she was trying to see. "Well . . . ?"

"Say it again," he said.

"If," she said, after a long pause, "if you could fall in love with your wife again . . . *would* you?"

"What a strange question."

"Not so strange. This of the best of all possible worlds, if the world ran the way worlds *should* run. Wouldn't it make sense, finally, for people to fall in love again and live happily ever after? After all, you were once wildly in love with Anne."

"Wildly."

"You can never forget that."

"Never. Agreed."

"Well, then, that being true—would you—"

"*Could* would be more like it."

"Forget about could. Let's imagine new circumstances, everything running right for a change, your wife behaving the way you describe her once-perfection instead of the way she acts now. What *then*?"

He leaned up on his elbow and looked at her.

"You're in a strange mood tonight. What gives?"

"I don't know. Maybe it's tomorrow. I'm forty, next month you're forty-two. If men go mad at forty-two, shouldn't women become sane two years earlier? Or maybe I'm thinking, What a shame. What a shame people don't fall in love and stay in love with the same people all their lives, instead of having to find others to be with, laugh with or cry with; what a shame . . ."

He reached over and touched her cheek and felt a wetness there. "Good grief, you're crying."

"Just a little bit. It's so damned sad. We are. *They* are. Everybody. Everyone. Sad. Was it always this way?"

"And hidden, I think. Nobody said."

"I think I envy those people a hundred years ago."

"Don't envy what you can't even guess. There was a lot of quiet madness under their serene no-talk."

He leaned over and kissed the tears from under her eyes, lightly.

"Now, what brought all this on?"

She sat up and didn't know what to do with her hands.

"What a joke," she said. "Neither you nor I smoke. In books and movies, when people lie in bed after, they light cigarettes." She put her hands across her breast and held on, as she talked. "It just, I was thinking of good old Robert, good old Bob, and how crazy I was for him once, and what am I doing here, loving you, when I should be home minding my thirty-seven-year-old-baby husband?"

"And?"

"And I was thinking how much I really, truly like Anne. She's a great woman; do you know that?"

"Yes, but I try not to think of it, everything considered. She's not you."

"But what if, suddenly"—she clasped her hands around her knees and fixed him with a bright, clear-blue gaze—"what if she *were* me?"

"I *beg* your pardon?" He blinked.

"What if all the qualities you lost in her and found in me were somehow given back to her? Would you, could you, love her all over again?"

"Now I really do wish I smoked!" He dropped his feet out onto the floor and kept his back to her, staring out the window. "What's the use of asking that kind of question, when there can never be an answer!?"

"That is the problem, though, isn't it?" She addressed his back. "You have what my husband lacks and I have what your wife lacks. What's needed is a double soul—no, a double heart transplant!" She almost laughed and then, deciding against it, almost cried.

"There's an idea there for a story, a novel, maybe a film."

"It's our story and we're sunk with it, and no way out, unless—"

"Unless?"

She got up and moved restlessly about the room, then went to stand and look out at the stars in the summer night sky.

"What makes it so rough is Bob's beginning to treat me the way he once treated me. The last month he's been so . . . fine, so terrific."

"Oh, my God." He sighed and shut his eyes.

"Yes. Oh, my God."

There was a long silence. At last, he said, "Anne's been acting better, too."

"Oh, my God," she repeated, in a whisper, shutting her own eyes. Then, at last, she opened them and traced the stars. "What's the old thing? 'If wishes were horses, beggars would ride'?"

"You've lost me for the third or fourth time in as many minutes."

She came and knelt on the floor by him and took both of his hands in hers and looked into his face.

"My husband, your wife are both out of town tonight, yes, at the far ends of the country, one in New York, the other in San Francisco. Correct? And you're sleeping over in this hotel room with me and we have all night together, but—" She stopped, searched, located and then tried the words: "But what if, just before we go to sleep, what if we made a kind of mutual wish, me for you, you for me?"

"A *wish*?" He started to laugh.

"Don't." She shook his hands. He quieted. She went on: "A wish that while we slept, somehow, by a miracle, please God, please all the Graces and Muses and magical times and great dreams, somehow, some way, we would both"—she slowed and then continued—"both fall back in love, you with your wife, me with my husband."

He said nothing.

"There," she said.

He reached over, found some matches on the side table, struck one, and held it up to light her face. The fire glowed in her eyes and would not go away. He exhaled. The match went out.

"I'll be damned," he whispered. "You *mean* it."

"I do, and we *are*. Damned, that is. Would you *try*?"

"Lord—"

"Don't say Lord as if I had gone crazy on you."

"Look—"

"No, you look." She took his hands again and pressed them, hard. "For me. Would you do me the favor? And I'd do the same for you."

"Make a wish?"

"We often did, as kids. They sometimes worked. They worked because they weren't really wishes, they were prayers."

He lowered his eyes. "I haven't prayed in years."

"Yes, you have. Count the times you wish you were back in the first month of your marriage. That's a kind of forlorn wish, a lost prayer."

He looked at her and swallowed several times.

"Don't say anything," she said.

"Why not?"

"Because right now, you feel you have nothing to say."

"I'll be quiet, then. Let me think. Do you, God, do you really want me to make a wish for you?"

She sank back and sat on the floor, her hands in her lap, eyes shut. Quietly, tears began to slide down her cheeks.

"Dear, oh, my dear," he said softly.

IT WAS THREE in the morning and the talking was done and they had ordered some hot milk and drunk it and brushed their teeth, and now, as he came out of the bathroom, he saw her arranging the pillows on the bed, as if this were a special new theater in a special new time.

"What am I doing here?" he said.

She turned. "Once we used to know. Now we don't. Come along." She gestured and patted his side of the bed.

He rounded the bed. "I feel silly."

"You have to feel silly just so you can feel better." She pointed at the bed.

He got in and put his head on the properly plumped pillow and folded the sheets neatly over his chest and clasped his hands on the sheets.

"Does this look right?" he asked.

"Perfect. Now."

She put out the light and slid in on her side and took one

of his hands and lay back perfectly straight and neat on her pillow.

"Feeling tired, feeling sleepy?"

"Enough," he said.

"All right, then. Be serious now. Don't say anything. Just think. You know what."

"I know."

"Shut your eyes now. There. Good."

She shut her own and they lay there, with just their hands clasped and nothing in the room now that stirred save their breathing.

"Take a breath," she whispered.

He took a breath.

"Now exhale."

He exhaled.

She did the same.

"Now," she murmured. "Begin." She whispered. *"Wish."*

Thirty seconds ticked by on their watches.

"Are you wishing?" she asked softly, at last.

"Wishing," he said, just as softly.

"Good," she whispered. And then: "Good night."

Perhaps a minute later, his quiet voice, inaudible, moved in the dark room:

"Goodbye."

HE AWOKE FOR no reason except that he had had a dream that the earth had shrugged, or an earthquake had happened ten thousand miles away that no one felt, or that there had been a second Annunciation but everyone was deaf, or perhaps it was only that the moon had come into the room during the night and changed the shape of the room and changed the looks on their faces and the flesh on their bones and now had stopped so abruptly that the quick silence had stirred his eyes wide. In the moment of opening, he knew the streets were dry, there had been no rain. Only, perhaps, some sort of crying.

And, lying there, he knew that somehow the wish had been granted.

He didn't know it immediately, of course. He sensed and guessed it because of an incredible new warmth in the room, nearby, which came from the lovely woman lying by his side.

The sureness, the regularity, the serene rise and fall of her breathing told him more. A spell had arrived, resolved itself, and passed straight on into truthful existence while she slept. Celebration was in her blood now, even though she was not awake to know it. Only her dream knew, and whispered it every time she exhaled.

He rose up onto his elbow, afraid to trust his intuition.

He bent to look at that face, more beautiful than he had ever known it.

Yes, the sign was there. The absolute certainty was there. The peace was there. The sleeping lips smiled. If her eyes had opened, they would have been blazing with light.

Wake up, he wanted to say. I know your happiness. Now you must discover it. Wake up.

He reached to touch her cheek but pulled his hand away. Her eyelids moved. Her mouth opened.

Quickly, he turned and lay huddled over on his side of the bed and waited.

After a long while, he heard her sit up. Then, as if struck a lovely blow, she exclaimed something, cried out, reached over, touched him, found him asleep, and sat beside him, discovering what he already knew.

He heard her get up and run around the room like a bird wishing to be free. She came and kissed him on the cheek, went away, came back, kissed him again, laughed softly, then went off quickly into the sitting room. He heard her dialing long distance and shut his eyes, tightly.

"Robert?" her voice said, at last. "Bob? Where are you? Silly. Stupid of me. I *know* where you are. Robert. Bob, oh, God, can I fly there, will you be there when I arrive, today, this afternoon, tonight, yes? Would it be all right? . . . What's come *over* me? I don't know. Don't ask. Can I come? Yes? Say yes! . . . Oh, grand! Goodbye!"

He heard the telephone click.

After a while, he heard her blowing her nose as she entered the room and sat on the bed next to him in the first light of dawn. She had dressed quickly and haphazardly, and now he reached out and took her hand.

"Something happened," he whispered.

"Yes."

"The wish. It came true."

"Isn't it incredible? Impossible, but it did! Why? How?"

"Because both of us believed," he said, quietly. "I wished very hard, for you."

"And I for you. Oh, Lord, isn't it wonderful that both of us could shift at the same time, move, change, all in a night? Otherwise, it would be terrible, wouldn't it, if just one changed and the other was left behind?"

"Terrible," he admitted.

"Is it really a miracle?" she asked. "Did we wish hard enough and someone or something or God heard us and lent us back our old loves to warm us and tell us to behave, we might never have another wish or another chance again, is that it?"

"I don't know. Do you?"

"Or was it just our secret selves knowing the time was over, a new time had come, and time for us to both turn around and go, is that the real truth?"

"All I know is I heard you on the phone just now. When you're gone, I'll call Anne."

"Will you?"

"I will."

"Oh, Lord, I'm so happy for you, for me, for us!"

"Get out of here. Go. Get. Run. Fly away home."

She jumped to her feet and banged at her hair with a comb and gave up, laughing. "I don't care if I look funny—"

"Beautiful," he corrected.

"Beautiful to you, maybe."

"Always and forever."

She came and bent down and kissed him and wept.

"Is this our last kiss?"

"Yes." He thought about it. "The last."

"One more, then."

"Just one."

She held his face in her hands and stared into it.

"Thanks for your wish," she said.

"Thanks for *yours*."

"You calling Anne right now?"

"Now."

"Best to Anne."

"Best to Bob. God love you, dear lady. Goodbye."

She was out the door and in the next room and the outside door shut and the hotel suite was very quiet. He heard her footsteps fade a long way off in the hall toward the elevator.

He sat looking at the phone but did not touch it.

He looked in the mirror and saw the tears beginning to stream unendingly out of his eyes.

"You, there," he said to his image. "You. Liar." And again: "Liar!"

And he turned and lay back down in the bed and put one hand out to touch that empty pillow there.

Quid Pro Quo

YOU DO NOT build a Time Machine unless you know where you are going. Destinations. Cairo after Christ? Macedonia before Methuselah? Hiroshima just before? Destinations, places, happenings.

But I built my Time Machine, all unknowingly, with no destination in mind, no happening about to arrive or, just this second, depart.

I built my Far Traveling Device with fragments of wired-together ganglion, the seat of invisible perception, of intuitive awareness.

An accessory to this inner side of the medulla oblongata and the brain shelves behind the optic nerve.

Between the hidden senses of the brain and the probing but invisible radar of the ganglion I ramshackled together a perceptor of future beings or past behaviors far different than name-places and mind-shaking events.

My Tin Lizzie watch, my dust invention, had microwave antennae with which to touch, find, and make moral judgments beyond my own intelligence

The Machine, in sum, would add up integers of human rise and fall and mail itself there to shape destinies, taking me along as blind baggage.

Did I know this as I pasted and screwed and welded my seemingly hapless mechanical child? I did not. I simply tossed forth notions and needs, opinions and predictions based on successes and failures, and at the end stood back to stare at my useless creation.

For there it stood in my attic, a bright object, all angles and elbows, purring, anxious for travel but going nowhere unless I begged "go" instead of "sit" or "stay." I would not give it directions; I would simply at the right time shed my "ambiance," my soul's light, upon it.

Then it would rear up and gallop off in all directions. Arriving where, only God knew.

But we would know when we arrived.

So there is the start of it all.

A strange dream lurking in a dim attic, with two seats for Tourists, a bated breath and a bright hum of its spidery nerves.

Why had I built it in my attic?

After all, it wouldn't sky-dive midair, but only hang-glide Time.

The Machine. Attic. Waiting. For what?

Santa Barbara. A small bookshop, and my signing a small novel for an even smaller group when the explosion occurred. Which hardly describes the force with which it slammed me back on my inner wall.

It began when I glanced up and saw this old, old man swaying in the doorway, dreading to enter. He was incredibly wrinkled. His eyes were broken crystal. Saliva brimmed his trembling lips. He shook as if lightning struck him when he gaped his mouth and gasped.

I went back to signing books until an intuitive cog slipped in my head. I glanced up again.

The old, old man still hung there like a scarecrow, framed against the light, his head thrust forward, eyes aching for recognition.

My body froze. I felt the blood run cold along my neck and down my arms. The pen fell from my fingers as the old, old man lurched forward, giggling, hands groping.

"Remember me?" he cried, laughing.

I searched the long frazzled gray hair that blew about his cheeks, noted the white chin stubble, the sun-bleached shirt, the half-soiled denims, the sandals on his bony feet, then up again to his demon eyes.

"Do you?" he smiled.

"I don't think—"

"Simon Cross!" he exploded.

"Who?"

"Cross!" he bleated. "I am Simon Cross!"

"Son of a bitch!" I reared back.

My chair fell. The small crowd fell back, too, as if struck. The old, old man, riven, shut his eyes, flinching.

"Bastard!" Tears leaped to my eyes. "Simon Cross? What have you done with your life!?"

Eyes clenched, he lifted his gnarled and shivering hands, palms out, horribly empty to wait for my further cry.

"Sweet Jesus," I said. "Your life. What did you do to it?"

With a great thunderclap my memory reversed to forty years lost, forty years gone, and myself, thirty-three, at the start of my own career.

And Simon Cross stood before me, nineteen years old and handsome to the point of beauty with a bright face, clear and innocent eyes, an amiable demeanor, his bones relaxed within his flesh, and a bundle of story manuscripts under his arm.

"My sister said—" he began.

"I know, I know," I interrupted. "I read your stories last night, the ones she gave me. You're a genius."

"I wouldn't say that," said Simon Cross.

"I would. Bring more stories. Without looking I can sell every one of them. Not as an agent, but a friend to genius."

"Don't say that," said Simon Cross.

"I can't help myself. Someone like you lives once in a lifetime."

I riffled through his new stories.

"Oh, God, yes, yes. Beautiful. Sell them all, and take no commission."

"I'll be damned," he said.

"No, blessed. Genetically blessed, by God."

"I don't go to church."

"You don't need to," I said. "Now, get out of here. Let me

get my breath. Your genius is blasphemy to plain dogs like me. I admire, envy, and almost hate you. Go!"

And he smiled a bewildered smile and got out, left me with his white-hot pages burning my hand, and within two weeks I had sold every one of these tales by a nineteen-year-old man-child whose words walked him on water and flew him midair.

The response quaked the earth across country.

"Where did you find this writer?" some said. "He reads like the bastard son of Emily Dickinson out of Scott Fitzgerald. You his agent?"

"No. He'll need no agent."

And Simon Cross wrote a dozen more stories that leaped from his machine into print and acclaim.

Simon Cross. Simon Cross. Simon Cross.

And I was his honorary father, visionary discoverer, and envious but forgiving friend.

Simon Cross.

And then, Korea.

And him standing on my front porch in a pure salt-white sailor's suit, his face still unshaven, his cheeks sunburned, his eyes drinking the world, a last story in his hands.

"Come back, dear boy," I said.

"I'm not a boy."

"No? God's forever child then, burning bright! Stay alive. Don't become too famous."

"I won't." He hugged me and ran.

Simon Cross. Simon Cross.

And the war over and the time lost and him vanished. Spend ten years here, thirty there, and just rumors of my wandering genius child. Some said he had landed in Spain, married a castle, and championed dove shooting. Others swore they had seen him in Morocco, perhaps Marrakech. Spend another swift decade and jump the sill into 1998 with a Travel Machine treading useless waters in your attic and all Time on your hands, and book-signing fans pressed close when cracking the silence of forty years, what?!

Simon Cross. Simon Cross.

"Damn you to hell!" I shouted.

The old, old man railed back, frightened, hands shielding his face.

"Damn you!" I cried. "Where have you been? How have you used yourself? Christ, what a waste! Look at you! Straighten up! Are you who you say you are?"

"I—"

"Shut up! God, you stupid nerveless monster, what have you done to that fine young man?"

"What fine young man?" the old, old one babbled.

"You. *You.* You were the genius. You had the world by the tail. You wrote upside down backwards and it all came right! The world was your oyster. You made pearls. Christ, do you know what you've done?"

"Nothing."

"Yes! Nothing! And all you had to do was whistle, blink, and it was yours!"

"Don't hit me!" he cried.

"Hit you? Kill you, maybe! Hit you! My God!"

I looked around for a blunt instrument. I had only my fists, which I stared at and dropped in despair.

"Don't you know what life is, you damned idiot fool?" I said at last.

"Life?" gasped the old, old man.

"It's a deal. A deal you make with God. He gives you life, and you pay back. No, not a gift, a loan. You don't just take, you give. Quid pro quo!"

"Quid—?"

"Pro quo! One hand washes the other. Borrow and repay, give and take. And you! What a waste! My God, there are ten thousand people out there who'd kill for your talent, who'd die to be what you were and now aren't. Lend me your body, give me your brain, if you don't want it, give it back, but my God, run it to ruin? Lose it forever? How could you? What made you? Suicide and murder, murder and suicide! Oh damn, damn, damn you to hell!"

"Me?" gasped the old, old man.

"Look!" I cried, and spun him to face a shop mirror and see his own shipwreck. "Who is that?"

"Me," he bleated.

"No, that's the young man you lost! Damn!"

I raised my fists and it was a moment of stunned release. Images knocked my mind: Suddenly the attic loomed and the useless Machine waiting for no purpose. The Machine I had dreamed wondering why, for what? The Machine with two chairs waiting for occupants going where?

My fists, midair, froze. The attic flashed in my mind and I lowered my fists. I saw the wine on the signing table and took it up.

"Were you going to hit me?" the old, old man cried.

"No. Drink this."

He opened his eyes to the glass in his hand.

"Does it make me larger or smaller?" he said inanely.

Alice down the rabbit hole with the DRINK ME bottle that grew her outsize or dwarf-small.

"Which?" he said.

"Drink!"

He drank. I refilled the glass. Astounded at this gift confounding my fury, he drank and drank a third and his eyes wet with surprise.

"What?"

"This," I said, and dragged him half-crippled out to the car and slung him in like a scarecrow and was off down the road, myself grimly silent, Simon Cross, the lost son of a bitch, babbling.

"Where?"

"Here!"

We swerved into my front drive. I yanked him inside and up into the attic without breaking his neck.

We stood, imbalanced, by my Time Machine.

"Now I know why I built it." I said.

"Built what?" cried Simon Cross.

"Shut up. In!"

"An electric chair?"

"Maybe. Jump!"

He jumped and I locked him in place and took the second seat and threw the control lever.

"What?" said Simon Cross.

"No," I said. "Where!"

Swiftly, I hit the tabs: year/month/day/hour/minute; and just as swiftly: state/town/street/block/number; and yanked the backward/turn/backward bar.

And we were off, dials spinning, unspinning suns, moons, and years until the Machine melted to silence.

Simon Cross, stunned, glanced around.

"Why," he said, "this is my place."

"Your home, yes."

I dragged him up the front walk.

"And there, yes, there, do you see?" I said.

On the front porch, in his sunbright sailor's suit, stood the beautiful young man with a clutch of story pages in his hands.

"That's me!" cried the old, old man.

"You. Simon Cross."

"Hello," said the young man in the fresh white sailor's suit. He scowled at me, curious, then puzzled. "Hold on. Why do you look—different?" He nodded at his older self. "And who's this?"

"Simon Cross," I said.

In silence, youth looked at age, age looked at youth.

"That's not Simon Cross," said the young man.

"That can't be me," said the old one.

"Yes."

Slowly, both turned to look at me.

"I don't understand," said Simon Cross, nineteen years old.

"Take me back!" the old man exclaimed.

"Where?"

"To where we were, wherever that was," he gasped wildly.

"Go away." The young man backed off.

"I can't," I said. "Look close. This is what you will become after you've lost yourself. Simon Cross, yes, forty years on."

The young sailor stood for a long moment, his eyes searching up and down the old man's body and fixing on his eyes. The young sailor's face reddened. His hands became fists, relaxed, became fists again. Words did not convince, but some intuition, some power unseen, an invisible vibration between the old man and himself.

"Who are you really?" he said at last.

The old, old man's voice broke.

"Simon Cross."

"Son of a bitch!" cried the young man. "Damn you!"

And struck a blow to the older man's face, and then another and another and the old, old man stood in the rain, the downpour of blows, eyes shut, drinking the violence, until he fell on the pavement with his young self astride him staring at the body.

"Is he dead?" he wondered.

"You killed him."

"I had to."

"Yes."

The young man looked at me. "Am I dead, too?"

"Not if you want to live."

"Oh God, I do, I do!"

"Then get away from here. I'll take him with me, back to where we came from."

"Why are you doing this?" said Simon Cross, only nineteen.

"Because you're a genius."

"You keep saying that."

"True. Run, now. Go."

He took a few steps and stopped.

"Second chance?" he said.

"Oh, God, I hope so," I said.

And then added, "Remember this. Don't live in Spain or become the champion dove shooter in Madrid."

"I would never be a champion dove shooter anywhere!"

"No?"

"No!"

"And never become the old, old man I must drag through Time to meet himself."

"Never."

"You'll remember all this and live by it?"

"It's remembered."

He turned and ran down the street.

"Come," I said to the body, the scarecrow, the silent thing. "Let's get you in the Machine and find you an unmarked grave."

In the Machine, I stared up the .w empty street.

"Simon Cross," I whispered. "Godspeed."

And threw the switch and vanished in the future.

After
the Ball

SOMEWHERE ABOVE THE building whose flake-painted sign read MYRON'S BALLROOM the lights flickered as if to go out and a small orchestra of truly fragile size played "Good Night Ladies," and there was a murmur of regret and then a chorus of conversation and the rustle of bodies and shuffle of feet as shadows moved toward exits and the orchestra stopped and half the lights blinked and went out completely.

After a moment a side door opened below and the five—or was it six?—musicians emerged carrying their now-heavy instruments and loped to the only visible cars as if to avoid the larger flood of people talking and laughing, coming down the main staircase to the pavement. By the time the ballroom dancers, for that is what they were, touched ground by the dozens, and finally a hundred in all—sixty old women and an almost similar number of old men—the musicians' cars had long since sped off into a night with high fog above and a low fog coming in from the sea.

Roughly thirty of the celebrants lined up on the south side of the street awaiting rides on the inbound electric trolley, while the rest, somehow much louder and more jolly, waited across for the larger big train-size trolley that would charge and bang them off toward the Pacific Ocean shore.

Lined up and beginning to shiver in the late-night always-familiar California air (it had been 85 degrees at noon), the men cursed while the ladies in flower-print evening gowns peered down the tracks imbedded in asphalt as if staring would bring locomotion.

Which, miraculously, it did.

"There, see!" cried the ladies.

"I'll be damned," said the men.

And all the while, not looking at each other, even when the huge cross-country-size double car train pulled up in sparks and brake steam, the men in their perspiration-crumpled tuxes helped the evening-dressed women up the iron steps without glancing at their faces.

"Upsy-daisy."

"There we go."

"Atsa girl."

And the men clambered on like castaways, at the last moment leaping aboard.

With a clang of bell and a horn blow, the huge cross-continental train, only going to Venice, thirty miles away, cast all adrift and bucketed toward a one-o'clock-in-the-morning perdition.

To the clamoring delight of ladies exhausted with inexpensive joy, and men longing to dislodge the stiff white shirtfronts and unstrangle their ties.

"It's hot, throw the windows up!"

"It's cold, put the windows down!"

And then, with equal parts arctic and equal parts equatorial, the old children of late Saturday plunged toward a sea with no icebergs, a shore with wild hopes.

In the first car, a man and woman sat just behind a motorman deeply influenced by orchestra conductor's baton gymnastics, as he rapped the brass handles left, right, between, and glared out at a fog without cars, from which at any moment some wreck might fully wreck itself.

Steel on steel, the train thundered them safely off from Myron's toward Neptune's.

For a long while the couple sat silently swaying until at last, watching the motorman's acrobatics, the woman of some years said, "Let me sit by the window, do you mind?"

"No, no, please, I was going to suggest that."

She slid in along the hard wooden bench and gazed out the window at the dark buildings passing and the night trees, and only a few stars, and barely a sliver moon this night, this month.

"What are you thinking?" he asked.

The shadows passed, the shadows passed, the shadows passed.

"You ever think," she said, quietly, half-seeing her silhouette, also a shadow, on the window glass, "my land, being in a rickety old wreck of a train like this, making such a racket on the track, is like being a kind of traveler, I mean in time, we're going back, not ahead."

"I never thought that," he said, trying to crane around so he could see her clearly, but her head was pretty well turned to the window, which seemed like a TV window with stations coming and going, unfocused, channels changing every second. He looked down at his white-gloved hands. "Never thought."

"Well, think it," she murmured.

"What?"

"Think it," she said, more clearly.

"And another thing," she said, just as quietly, watching the passing night TV stations on their own quick circuits, come and gone. "This isn't only a time-and-place means of transportation. I feel something else."

"What?"

"Feel like I'm sort of melting away, I don't know, kind of losing weight, the more we move, the further we go, I feel lighter, down some pounds and then more, isn't that strange. You feel that?"

"I don't think so."

"Go ahead, feel it, take your time. Relax. Doesn't it sort of just come up out of your feet, your ankles, get to your knees, so you feel, I don't know, let loose? You kind of hang inside your clothes."

He puzzled for a long moment, tried to look over her

shoulder again, but all he saw in the colorless window glass was the silhouette, a face with no visible features.

"Go ahead," she murmured. "Relax. Let yourself go. Take it easy. Well?"

"I sort of feel it." He sat back, head down, examining his knees and the shirt cuffs half shot out of his coat sleeves.

"Don't talk about it, just, nice and easy, do it," she said, not turning.

"Yeah," he said, turning his gloved hands over and then back down on his knees, massaging. "Almost."

"Don't lie."

"No, no," he insisted quickly. "Why would I lie?"

"Men always do. They're good at it. Put in a lifetime at it. Get good by now."

"No, no," he said. "I feel it."

"Good boy," she said. "Keep quiet now and feel it more. There. There. You see?"

He nodded rather than reply. The big red car trolley train rocketed out of one small area of houses and buildings into and through an open field and then a few more nurseries, and then empty land moving toward yet another small community near the sea.

"You're pretty good," he said admiringly.

"Shh," she hissed.

"No, but I mean," he whispered, "you'd be the life of the party, telling people things, giving them ideas, half putting them to sleep, saying 'do this,' 'do that,' and they do it. I'm losing weight, like you said."

"Good," she said. "Shh."

He glanced around uneasily at all the night celebrants, swaying in the motion of the train, traveling a long way in a short distance.

"You ever notice," he tried, "every single person, every one, every woman, every man this evening is wearing white gloves. You, me, everyone."

"I wonder why?" she said, turned away.

"You got me."

The train plummeted on into gathering mist and then wisps of fog, and he sat rocking back and forth with the sway of the big wooden-floored car and looked at the back of her neck where the tender dark curls gathered and at last said: "Your name. Out on the dance floor, you said, but the band played so loud—"

Her lips moved.

"Beg pardon?" he said.

Her lips moved again and then a final time.

"Here we are," she said.

"My name, now," he said, "is—"

"Here we are," she said, and brushed past him and was half up the aisle to the door before he sensed she was gone and the train was slowing. He saw a few lights outside, and the door hissed open before he could proceed her and help her down into the dark. But at last he stood beside her as the great night train pulled away with a bell and horn and he looked to see her standing motionless, looking up at the sky.

"We'd better not stand here in the middle of the street," he said. "Traffic."

"There are no cars," she responded, calmly, and began to walk.

She was half across the street before he caught up.

"I was just saying," he said.

"A night with no moon, that makes me glad. There's true romance for you. A night with no moon."

"I thought moons and moonlight were—"

But she cut him off. "No moon, no light. The best."

And she was up over the curb and along the walk and turning in at her place, which was upstairs, one fourth of a fourplex.

"Quiet as a mouse," she murmured.

"Yes!"

"Keep your voice down."

"Yes," he whispered, and they were inside at the staircase and he saw that she was removing her shoes and glancing at him, so he did the same. She moved up to the first tread, soundless, and looked to see he was carrying her shoes, nodded and repeated, "Like mice."

And she ascended in a soundless glide with him fumbling after. When he got to the top she was already in her apartment, a large parlor with a double bed in its middle, and beyond, a small dining room and a kitchen. The door closed on the bathroom, soundless.

After a moment she called out, very quietly, "Don't stand there," which he interpreted as meaning off with the tuxedo coat and after some hesitation the white shirtfront and collar and after another long while, unlatching his suspenders and folding them and his pants over a chair that he found in the shadowed room, lit only by a small nightlight and a lamp on the far side of the bed. Standing there in a half shirt and his black socks and underwear, he wavered and dodged about going in one direction, then the other, moving toward the bed and backing away, with no map, no guide, no late-night instructions.

"Are you where you're supposed to be?" she asked quietly behind the door. He gazed at the bed.

"Are you?" she prompted, almost inaudibly.

He went to the bed and said, "I think so," and got in and one of the wire springs sang softly.

"You are," she said.

The bathroom door opened. A tall silhouette was there. Before he could see her clearly, the light went out and a shadow crossed the room.

"Eyes shut?"

He nodded, numbly. He felt her weight upon the bed and heard the sheets part and whisper as she drifted in.

"Open your eyes."

He opened them but it was the same as on the train, where, turned away, he saw only a silhouette cutout, and here, though she faced toward him, she blocked the lamp so the lamp made her a hillock of shadow with no features. He tried to find her face, he knew it was there, but his eyes wouldn't focus.

"Good evening," she said.

"Evening."

And after a moment as she gained her breath and he did the same, she said, "My, that was a long trip."

"Too long. I could hardly wait—"

"Don't say," she said.

He looked at the long shadow and the pale face with dim outlines of features.

"But . . ."

"Don't say," she said.

He held his breath for he knew she would go on in a moment. She did.

"Teachers say if you write a story you must never name what you're trying to write. Just do it. When it's over you'll know what you've done. So . . . don't say."

It was the most she had said all evening. Now she fell silent, a shadow against the light. And now the lamp went dark without, it seemed, her turning to touch it. He saw the merest gesture in the shadows. Something soft fell to the floor. It was a moment before he realized it was her gloves. She had taken off her gloves.

Surprised, he sensed that the only thing that he still wore was his gloves. But when he tried to work them off he found that he had already tossed them aside in the dark. Now his hands were revealed and vulnerable. He pulled back.

He opened his mouth but she stopped him. "Don't say anything."

He felt her move a small move, toward him.

"Say only one thing."

He nodded, wondering what it would be.

"Tell me," she said very quietly. He could not make out her face, it was still like the face in the window glass on the night train, traveling from station to station, a dark silhouette fixed between late-night TV channels, and pale and hidden.

"Tell me," she said. He nodded. "How *old* are you?"

His mouth gaped. He felt his eyes panic in his head. She repeated the question, implying the answer. Suddenly he absolutely knew the right and amazing truth. He shut his eyes, cleared his throat, and at last let his tongue move.

"I'm . . ." he said.

"Yes?"

"I'm eighteen, nineteen in August, five feet eight, one hundred fifty pounds, brown hair, blue eyes. Unattached."

He imagined he heard her very softly echo every word that he had said.

He felt her shift, weightless, closer and still closer.

"Say that again," she whispered.

In Memoriam

ALL THE WAY home that late afternoon, driving through the winding streets, enjoying the weather, admiring the jacaranda trees and the violet snow they were letting down on the lawns, he noticed, but merely from the corner of his eyes, the apparatuses in front of almost every other garage. But they passed behind him without being named. They were familiar but there was no special reason to give them notice.

The basketball hoops and boards above the garages, waiting for games.

Nothing special. No particular connotations.

Until he drove up in front of his house in the autumn weather and saw his wife standing, arms folded, out on the sidewalk, watching a young man up on a stepladder, his hands busy with a screwdriver and hammer. Neither noticed him until he banged the car. The young man looked down and his wife looked over as he gave a surprising cry.

"What the hell goes on?" he shouted, and was amazed at his own emotion. His wife gave a calm response.

"Why, we're just taking it down, is all. It's been up there for years, and . . ."

The husband glared up along the ladder.

"Get down off there," he said.

"Why?" his wife said.

"I don't have to have a reason, dammit, get down!"

The young man nodded, rolled his eyeballs to heaven, and climbed down.

"Now put the ladder away!" the husband said.

"You don't have to shout," his wife said.

"Am I? Well. Just put the ladder away. Thanks."

"That's more like it," she said.

The young man carried the ladder into the open garage and left, quietly, in his car.

The husband and wife, during all this, stood in the middle of the driveway gazing up at the basketball hoop.

When the car was gone, she said, "Now what's all this about?"

"You know!" he cried, and lowered his voice. "Hell." He looked at his hands, on which had fallen a surprise of tears. "What's this?"

"If you don't know, no one does." She softened her voice. "Come inside."

"Not until we finish."

"The ladder's gone and the hoop stays up. For now, anyway."

"No, not for now," he said, doggedly. "From now *on*."

"But why?"

"I want it there. Just in case."

"In case what?"

"There's got to be one place in all the damned world that's his. There's nothing out at the graveyard. There's nothing anywhere in this country. Nothing in Saigon, especially Saigon. So, when I look up at this, hell, you know what I mean."

She looked up at the net and the hoop.

"Next thing you'll put flowers—"

"Don't make jokes!"

"I'm sorry. It's just—you won't let go."

"Why should I?"

"For your own good."

"What about his good?"

"I don't know the answer. Do *you*?"

"It'll come. God, I'm sick to my stomach. Where's the damn ladder, I'll knock it all down."

She stared at him so he wandered into the garage and rummaged among newspapers and discovered the basketball, looked out at the hoop, but did not bring the ball out.

She called into the unlit garage.

"You hungry?"

"No," he said tiredly. "I guess."

"I'll fix something." He heard her walk to the front porch. As the door was shutting, he said, "Thanks."

He walked out to stand under the hoop and watched the wind shake the net.

"Why?" he said quietly. "Why in hell?"

He glanced along the street west and then along the street east. Down both ways there were garage fronts with basketball boards and hoops, stirred by the same wind, never removed, some for one reason, some for another.

He counted two on one side of the street, and three on the other.

What a great way, he thought, to know what kind of families live in those houses.

He stood for a long while until he felt his wife move behind the front screen door, then he shut the garage door and went in.

There was wine with dinner, not often observed. She filled his glass twice and waited.

"Forgive me," she said at last. "But you do realize, don't you? He's never coming back."

"Don't!" he said, and pushed his chair back and put his knife and fork down.

"Someone's got to say it."

"No they don't."

"We said it all before. It's been years."

"I don't care how many years."

She looked down at her plate and said, "Drink your wine."

"I will when I feel like it." At last he picked up the glass. "Anyway, thanks." He drank.

After a long silence she said, "How much longer will this go on?"

"Now that you've started it up again?"

"I didn't mean to start it up. I just got out the ladder and hired some help."

"You just didn't figure, is all."

"It's just," she said, "you haven't slept well lately. I thought maybe if I—well, I wanted to find a way to help you rest. That's not so bad, is it? You're worn out."

"Am I?" He felt his knees and nodded. "Yes. I am."

"It must be," she said, at last, "you're waiting for something. What?"

"I wish I knew." He picked up his fork but did not eat. "It's just last night and the night before I listened."

"For what?"

"Something. I must have lain there for an hour, just listening. Waiting. But there was nothing."

"Eat. You're starving."

"Yes, but starving for what?"

"Here," she said. "Finish the wine."

At bedtime she said, "Try to sleep."

"You can't *try* sleeping, it's got to *happen*."

"Try anyway," she said. "I worry." She kissed his cheek and went to the bedroom door.

"I'll be in in a minute," he said.

Far across town he heard a single university bell chime midnight, and then one, and then two o'clock. He sat with an unread book in his lap and a new bottle of wine to one side, eyes shut, waiting. The wind outside rose.

Finally when the distant bell sounded three, he got up and

walked out the front door and opened the garage. He went in and stood for a long moment, regarding the basketball. He did not carry it out in the light but simply let it sit on the cement floor.

If I leave the garage door open, he thought, *that* should do it.

He went out and almost glanced up at the net, but thought, Don't look. Don't notice. That way, maybe—

He shut his eyes and turned to just stand there in the moonlight, listening, aching to hear, swaying slightly, but not once opening his eyes to look up at the board and the hoop and the net.

The wind shivered in the trees.

Yes, he thought.

A leaf blew across the drive.

Yes, he thought, oh, yes.

A soft sound rose, like someone running a long way off and then, nearer, walking, and then nothing.

And after a while a motion around him and other sounds, some fast, some slow, circling.

Yes, he thought. Oh God yes.

And, eyes shut, he reached out both hands to feel the air, but there was only wind and moonlight.

Yes, he thought. Now.

And again: *Now.*

And yet again: *Now.*

At dawn his wife came to sit on his bed. The motion wakened him. He looked up at her face.

"It's gone," she said.

"What?"

She glanced away to the front window.

He rose slowly and moved to the window and stared down at the front of the garage.

There was no board, no hoop, no net.

"What happened last night?" she said.

"Something."

"What?"

"I don't know. The weather maybe. The moon moving made things move and I asked *all* of it *what*?"

His wife waited, her hands in her lap.

"And?"

"Okay, I said, whoever you are, whatever this is, if we play one last game, can I sleep? One last game? I could feel the weather on my face and along my arms. The moon went out and came back. That was the sign. I moved. The weather moved."

"And then?"

"*We* played a last game."

"I thought I heard." She took a deep breath. "Who won?"

"*We* did," he said.

"You both can't win."

"You can. If you try."

"And you both won."

"Both."

She came to stand with him and study the empty garage front.

"Did *you* take it down?"

"Someone did."

"I didn't hear you get the ladder."

"I must've. It was hard climbing up, but even harder climbing down. My eyes kept filling up. I couldn't see."

"Where did you put all that stuff?" she said.

"Don't know. We'll find it when we least expect."

"Thank God it's over."

"Over, yes, but best of all—"

"What?"

"A tie," he said.

And repeated, "A tie."

Tête-à-Tête

WE WERE WALKING along the boardwalk in Ocean Park one summer evening, arm in arm, my friend Sid and me, when we saw a familiar sight on one of the benches just ahead, not far from the surf.

"Look," I said, "and listen."

We looked and listened.

There was this old Jewish couple, he I would say about seventy and she maybe sixty-five, moving their mouths and hands at the same time, everyone talking, nobody listening.

"I told you more than once," he said.

"What did you tell? Nothing!" she said.

"Something," he said, "I'm always telling you something. Of great importance if you'd give a try."

"Great importance, listen to him!" she said rolling her eyes. "Give me a list!"

"Well, about the wedding . . ."

"*Still* the wedding?"

"Sure! The waste, the confusion."

"*Who* was confused?"

"I could show you—"

"Don't show. Look, I'm deaf!"

Et cetera, et cetera.

"I wish I had a tape recorder," I said.

"Who needs a tape recorder," Sid replied. "I could say what I just heard. Call me at three in the morning and I'll quote."

We moved on. "They've been sitting on that same bench every night for years!"

"I believe it," said Sid. "They're hilarious."

"You don't find it sad?"

"Sad? Come off it! They're a vaudeville team. I could put them on the Orpheum circuit tomorrow!"

"Not even a *little* sad?"

"Stop. I bet they're married fifty years. The yammer started before the wedding and kept going after their honeymoon."

"But they don't *listen*!"

"Hey, they're taking *turns*! First hers not to listen, then his. If they ever paid attention they'd freeze. They'll never wind up with Freud."

"Why not?"

"They're letting it all hang out, there's nothing left to carp or worry about. I bet they get into bed arguing and are asleep with smiles in two minutes."

"You actually *think* that?"

"I had an aunt and uncle like that. A few insults shape a long life."

"How long did they live?"

"Aunt Fannie, Uncle Asa? Eighty, eighty-nine."

"*That* long?"

"On a diet of words, distemper almost, Jewish badminton—he hits one, she hits it back, she hits one, *he* hits it back, nobody wins but, hell, no one loses."

"I never thought of it that way."

"Think," said Sid. "Come on, it's time for refills."

We turned and strolled back on this fine summer night.

"And another thing!" the old man was saying.

"That's ten dozen other things!"

"Who's counting?" he said.

"Look. Where did I put that list?"

"Lists, who cares for lists?"

"Me. You don't, I do. Wait!"

"Let me finish!"

"It's never finished," Sid observed as we moved on and the great arguments faded in our wake.

Two nights later Sid called and said, "I got me a tape recorder."

"You mean?"

"You're a writer, I'm a writer. Let's trap a little grist for the mills."

"I dunno," I said.

"On your feet," said Sid.

We strolled. It was another fine mild California night, the

kind we don't tell Eastern relatives about, fearful they might believe.

"I don't want to hear," he said.

"Shut up and listen," she said.

"Don't tell me," I said, eyes shut. "They're still at it. Same couple. Same talk. Shuttlecock's always in the air over the net. No one's on the ground. You really going to use your tape recorder?"

"Dick Tracy *invented*, I *use*."

I heard the small handheld machine snap as we moved by, slowly.

"What was his name? Oh, yeah. Isaac."

"That wasn't his name."

"Isaac, sure."

"Aaron!"

"I don't mean Aaron, the older brother."

"Younger!"

"Who's telling this?"

"You. And bad."

"Insults."

"Truths you could never take."

"I got scars to prove it."

"Hot dog," said Sid as we glided on with their voices in his small device.

AND THEN IT happened. One, two, three, like that.

Quite suddenly the bench was empty for two nights.

On the third night I stopped into a small kosher delicatessen and talked, nodding at the bench. I didn't know the names. Sure, they said, Rosa and Al, Al and Rosa. Stein, they said, that was the name. Al and Rosa Stein, there for years, never missed a night. Now, Al will be missed. That was it. Passed away Tuesday. The bench sure looks empty, right, but what can you do?

I did what I could, prompted by an incipient sadness about two people I didn't really know, and yet I knew. From the small local synagogue I got the name of the almost smaller graveyard and for reasons confused and half-known went one late afternoon to look in, feeling like the twelve-year-old goy I once was, peering into the temple in downtown L.A., wondering what it was like to be part of all that chanting and singing, with all those men in hats.

In the graveyard I found what I knew I would find. The old woman was there, seated next to a stone bearing his name. And she was talking, talking, talking, touching the stone, talking to the stone.

And he? What else? Was not listening.

I waited, heard, shut my eyes and backed away.

With the sun gone and fog coming in with night I passed the bench. It was still empty, which made it worse.

So what can you do?

I called Sid.

"About that tape recorder of yours?" I said. "And some of those tapes?"

ON ONE OF the last nights of summer, Sid and I took our usual stroll down the kosher esplanade, passing the fine pastrami and cheesecake emporiums, stopped for some of that and walked on near the two dozen benches by the sea, talking and greatly contented, when Sid suddenly remarked, "You know, I have often wondered—"

"What's to wonder?" I said, for he was looking ahead at that bench, which had stayed empty for almost a week.

"Look." Sid touched my arm. "That old woman?"

"Yes?"

"She's back! I thought she was sick or something, but there she is."

"I know," I smiled.

"Since *when*? The same bench. And talking like crazy."

"Yes," I said, and we walked closer.

"But," said Sid as quiet as he could, "there's no one there. She's talking to *herself*."

"Almost," I said. We were very close. "Listen."

"You give me the same smarts. Arguments, who needs?" the old woman was saying, leaning forward toward the empty half of the bench, eyes fiery, face intense, mouth in full motion. "Arguments, who needs? I got plenty. Listen!"

And then, even more astonishing: a reply.

"Give a listen, she says!" a voice cried. "For what, how *come*?"

"That voice!" Sid exclaimed, then whispered. "*His* voice. But he's *dead*!"

"Yes," I said.

"And another thing," the old woman said, "look how you eat. Sometime, *watch!*"

"Easy for you to say!" the old man's voice shot back.

"Go ahead, *say!*"

There was a click. Sid's eyes slid down. He saw what I saw, his borrowed small handheld recorder in the old woman's palm.

"And another thing," she said, alive.

Click.

"Why do I put up with this?" his voice cried, dead.

Click.

"I got lists you wouldn't believe!" she cried, alive.

Sid glanced at me. "You?" he said.

"Me," I said.

"How?" Sid said.

"I had your tapes from all those nights," I said. "I cut them together, him talking, and put spaces between for her to yell back. Some places he just yells, no answer. Or she can click him off so she can yell, then click him back on."

"How did you know—?"

"She was in the graveyard," I said. "I couldn't stand it. Her just talking to that cold piece of marble and no answers. So I recopied your tapes, just his raves and yells, and one late afternoon looking into the graveyard I saw that yes, she was there and might be there forever and starve and die being there. No answers. But there *had* to be, even if you don't listen or think you don't, so I just walked in by the grave, turned on the tape, handed it to her where she sat by the stone, made sure he was yelling, and walked away. I didn't look back or wait to hear if she yelled, too. Him and her, her and him, high and low, low and high, I just left.

"Last night she was back here on the bench, eating some cheesecake. I think she's going to live. Isn't that swell?"

Sid listened. The old man was complaining. "Why do I put up with this? Someone *tell* me! I'm waiting. So?"

"Okay, smartie," the old woman cried.

Sid and I walked away in the late summer night. Her high voice and his deep voice faded.

Sid took my arm as we walked.

"For a goy," he said, "you make a fine Jew. What can I do you for?"

"Pastrami on rye?" I said.

The
Dragon Danced
at Midnight

REMEMBER THE AARON Stolittz jokes? How they called him the Vampire Bat because he was a fly-by-night producer? Remember his two studios? One a piano box, the other a cracker bin? I worked in the cracker bin near the Santa Monica graveyard. Great! Dead, you just moved ninety feet south to a good address.

Me? I plagiarized scripts, borrowed music, and edited film on *Monster, The Creature from Across the Hall* (my mother liked it, it resembled *her* mother), *The Mobile Mammoth*, and all the other Elephantine Aphid and Berserk Bacillus films we shot between sunset and sunrise the next day.

But all that changed. I lived through that great and awful night when Aaron Stolittz became world-famous, rich, and nothing was the same after that.

The phone rang early one hot September evening. Aaron

was up front in his studio. That is, he was hiding in one two-by-four office, beating vinegar-gnat sheriffs off the screen door. I was back splicing our latest epic film, using stolen equipment, when the phone buzzed. We jumped, afraid of bill-collector wives shrieking long-distance from forgotten years.

Finally, I lifted the receiver.

"Hey," a voice cried, "this is Joe Samasuku at the Samasuku Samurai Theater. Tonight at eight-thirty we scheduled a genuine Japanese surprise studio feature preview. But the film has been waylaid at a film festival in Pacoima or San Luis Obispo—who knows? Look. You got ninety minutes of film any way resembles a Samurai wide-screen or even a Chinese fairy tale? There's a fast fifty bucks in it. Give me the titles of your latest somebody-stepped-on-Junior-and-now-he-looks-better-than-ever pictures."

"*The Island of Mad Apes?*" I suggested.

Uneasy silence.

"*Two Tons of Terror?*" I went on.

The manager of the Samasuku Theater stirred to disconnect.

"*The Dragon Dances at Midnight!*" I cried impulsively.

"Yeah." The voice smoked a cigarette. "That *Dragon*. Can you finish shooting, cutting, and scoring it in . . . eh . . . one hour and thirty minutes?"

"Monster apple pie!" I hung up.

"*The Dragon Dances at Midnight?*" Aaron loomed behind me. "We got no such film."

"Watch!" I snapped some title letters under our camera. "As *The Island of Mad Apes* becomes *The Dragon Dances* et cetera!"

So I retitled the film, finished the music (old Leonard Bernstein outtakes run backward), and jockeyed twenty-four film reels into our Volkswagen. Usually films run nine reels, but, while editing, you keep film on dozens of short spools so it's easier to handle. There wasn't time to rewind our epic. The Samasuku would have to make do with a couple dozen cans.

We dented fenders roaring to the theater and ran the reels up to the projection booth. A man with a dire pirate's eye, and a breath like King Kong's, exhaled sherry wine, grabbed our reels, slammed and locked the metal door.

"Hey!" cried Aaron.

"Quick," I said. "After the show may be too late, let's go grab that fifty bucks and . . ."

"I'm ruined, ruined!" said a voice, as we went down the stairs.

Joe Samasuki, literally tearing his hair, stood staring at the mob as it jostled into the theater.

"Joe!" we both said, alarmed.

"Look," he groaned. "I sent telegrams warning them off. There's been a foul-up. And here comes *Variety, Saturday Review, Sight and Sound, Manchester Guardian, Avant-Garde Cinema Review*. Give me poisoned American food, go on!"

"Calmness, Joe," said Aaron. "Our film ain't all that bad."

"It's *not?*" I asked. "Aaron, those supersnobs! It's Hari-Kari Productions after tonight!"

"Calmness," said Aaron quietly, "is a drink we can buy in the bar next door. Come."

The film started with a great explosion of Dimitri Tiomkin themes upside down, backward, and super-reversed.

We ran for the bar. We were halfway through a double glass of serenity when the ocean crashed on the shore. That is to say, the audience in the theater gasped and sighed.

Aaron and I raced out, opened the theater door to gaze in at whatever dragon happened to be dancing that midnight.

I let out a small bleat, whirled, and leaped upstairs to beat on the projection-room door with my tiny fists. "Nincompoop! Louse! The reels are reversed. You got the number four reel in where it should be reel two!"

Aaron joined me, gasping, to lean against the locked door. "Listen!"

Behind the door a tinkling sound like ice and something that wasn't water.

"He's drinking."

"He's *drunk!*"

"Look," I said, sweating, "he's five minutes into the reel now. Maybe no one noticed. You, in there!" I kicked the door. "You're warned! Line 'em up! Get 'em right! Aaron," I said, leading him shakily downstairs, "let's buy you some more calmness."

We were finishing our second martini when another tidal wave hit the coastline.

I ran into the theater. I ran upstairs. I scrabbled at the projection-room peekhole. "Maniac! Destroyer! Not reel six! Reel three! Open up, so I can strangle you with my bare hands!"

He opened up . . . another bottle behind the metal door. I heard him stumble over tin cans of film strewn on the concrete floor.

Clawing my scalp, like a scene in *Medea*, I wandered back down to find Aaron gazing deep into his glass.

"Do all movie projectionists drink?"

"Do whales swim underwater?" I replied, eyes shut. "Does leviathan plumb the ocean seas?"

"Poet," said Aaron reverently. "Speak on."

"My brother-in-law," I spoke, "has been projectionist at TriLux Studios for fifteen years, which means fifteen years in which he has not drawn a sober breath."

"Think of that."

"I *am* thinking. Fifteen years seeing day after day the rushes for *Saddle of Sin*, the rerun of *Sierra Love Nest*, the recut of *Pitfall of Passion*. The concussion alone would give a man bends. Worse in long-run theaters. Imagine, the ninetieth time you see Carroll Baker in *Harlow*. Think, Aaron, think! Madness, huh? Up-the-wall panics. Sleepless midnights. Impotency. So? So you start drinking. All across night America at this very hour, conjure up the little settlements, the brave small forts, the big neon cities, and in every one, this second, Aaron, all the film projectionists, no exceptions, are drunker than hoot owl skunks. Drunk, drunk, drunk to a man."

We brooded over this and sipped our drinks. My eyes watered, imagining ten thousand projectionists alone with their films and bottles far across the prairie continent.

The theater audience stirred.

"Go see what that madman is doing now," said Aaron.

"I'm afraid."

The theater shook with a temblor of emotion.

We went out and stared up at the projection-room window above.

"He's got twenty-four reels of film there. Aaron, how many combinations can you put together out of that? Reel nine for reel five. Reel eleven for reel sixteen. Reel eight for reel twenty. Reel—"

"Stop!" Aaron groaned, and shuddered.

Aaron and I did not so much walk as run around the block.

We made it around six times. Each time we came back the shouts, squeals, and improbable roars of the crowd in the theater got louder.

"My God, they're ripping up the seats!"

"They wouldn't do that."

"They're killing their mothers!"

"Movie critics? You ever see their mothers, Aaron? Epaulettes down to here. Battle ribbons across to there. Work out at the gym five days a week. Build and launch battleships in their off-hours. Naw, Aaron, break each other's wrists, sure, but kill their *mothers* . . . ?"

There was a gasp, a hiss, a long-drawn sigh from the midnight dark within the California architecture. The big mission dome of the theater sifted dust.

I went in to stare at the screen until the reels changed. I came out.

"Reel nineteen in for reel ten," I said.

At which moment the theater manager staggered out, tears in his eyes, face all pale cheese, reeling from wall to wall with despair and shock.

"What have you done to me? What are you doing?" he shrieked. "Bums! Bastards! Ingrates! The Joe Samasuku Samurai Theater is ruined forever!"

He lunged at us, and I held him off. "Joe, Joe," I pleaded, "don't talk like that."

The music swelled. It was as if film and audience were inflating themselves toward a vast ripped-forth explosion which might tear mind from matter as flesh from bone.

Joe Samasuku fell back, pressed a key in my hand, and said, "Call the cops, telephone the janitor service to clean up after the riot, lock the doors if the doors are left, and don't call me, I'll call you!"

Then he fled.

We would have dogged him out of his old California patio and down the mean streets had not at that instant a huge stolen chunk of Berlioz and a cymbal smash straight out of Beethoven ended the film.

There was a stunned silence.

Aaron and I turned to stare madly at the shut-tight theater doors.

They banged wide open. The mob, in full cry, burst to view. It was a beast of many eyes, many arms, many legs, many shoes, and one immense and ever-changing body.

"I'm too young to die," Aaron remarked.

"You should've thought of that before you messed with things better left to God," said I.

The mob, the great beast, stopped short, quivering. We eyed it. It eyed us.

"There they are!" someone shouted at last. "The producer, the director!"

"So long, Aaron," I said.

"It's been great," said Aaron.

And the beast, rushing forward with an inarticulate cry, threw itself upon us . . . hoisted us to its shoulders and carried us, yelling happily, singing, slapping us on the back, three times around the patio, out into the street, then back into the patio again.

"Aaron!"

I stared down aghast into a swarming sea of beatific smiles. Here loped the reviewer of the *Manchester Guardian*. There bounded the mean and dyspeptic critic from the *Greenwich Village Avanti*. Beyond gamboled ecstasies of second-string film reviewers from *Saturday Review, The Nation*, and *The New Republic*. And far out on the shore of this tumultuous sea, in all directions, there was a frolic and jump, a laughing and waving of columnists from *Partisan Review, Sight and Sound, Cinema*, multitudinous beyond belief.

"Incredible!" they cried. "Marvelous! Superior to *Hiroshima Mon Amour*! Ten times better than *Last Year at Marienbad*! One hundred times greater than *Greed*! Classic! Genius! Makes *Giant* look like a Munchkin! My God, the New American Wave is in! How did you *do* it?"

"Do *what?*" I yelled, looking over at Aaron being carried for the fourth time around the lobby.

"Shut up and ride high in the saddle!" Aaron sailed over the ocean of humanity on a sea of smile.

I blinked up, wild strange tears in my eyes. And there in the projection-room window above, a shadow loomed with wide-sprung eyes. The projectionist, bottle in numbed hand, gasped down upon our revelry, ran his free fingers over his face in self-discovery, stared at the bottle, and fell away in shadow before I could shout.

When at last the hopping dancing dwarfs and gazelles were exhausted and laughing out their final compliments, Aaron and I were set back down on our feet with: "The most tremendous avant-garde film in history!"

"We had high hopes," said I.

"The most daring use of camera, editing, the jump-cut, and the multiple reverse story line I can remember!" everyone said at once.

"Planning pays off," said Aaron modestly.

"You're competing it in the Edinburgh Film Festival, of course?"

"No," said Aaron, bewildered, "we—"

"—planned on it after we show at the Cannes Film Festival competition," I cut in.

A battalion of flash cameras went off and, like the tornado that dropped Dorothy in Oz, the crowd whirled on itself and went away, leaving behind a litter of cocktail parties promised, interviews set, and articles that must be written tomorrow, next week, next month—remember, remember!

The patio stood silent. Water dripped from the half-dry

mouth of a satyr cut in an old fountain against the theater wall. Aaron, after a long moment of staring at nothing, walked over and bathed his face with water.

"The projectionist!" he cried, suddenly remembering.

We pounded upstairs and paused. This time we scratched at the tin door like two small, hungry white mice.

After a long silence a faint voice mourned, "Go away. I'm sorry. I didn't mean to do it."

"Didn't *mean* it? Hell, open up! All is forgiven." said Aaron.

"You're nuts," the voice replied faintly. "Go away."

"Not without you, honey. We love you. Don't we, Sam?"

I nodded. "We love you."

"You're out of your mother-minds."

Feet scraped tin lids and rattling film.

The door sprang open.

The projectionist, a man in his mid-forties, eyes bloodshot, face a furious tint of boiled-crab red, stood swaying before us, palms out and open to receive the driven nails.

"Beat me," he whispered. "Kill me."

"Kill you? You're the greatest thing that ever happened to dog meat in the can!"

Aaron darted in and planted a kiss on the man's cheek. He fell back, beating the air as if attacked by wasps, spluttering.

"I'll fix it all back just the way it was," he cried, bending to scrabble the strewn film snakes on the floor. "I'll find the right pieces and . . ."

"Don't!" said Aaron. The man froze. "Don't change a

thing," Aaron went on, more calmly. "Sam, take this down. You got a pencil? Now, you, what's your name?"

"Willis Hornbeck."

"Willis, Willie, give us the order. Which reels first, second, third, which reversed, upside down, backwards, the whole deal."

"You mean . . . ?" the man blinked, stupid with relief.

"I mean we got to have your blueprint, the way you ran the greatest avant-garde film in history tonight."

"Oh, for God's sake." Willis let out a hoarse, choking laugh, crouched among the tumbled reels, the insanely littered floor where his "art" lay waiting.

"Willis, honey," said Aaron. "You know what your title is going to be as of this hour of this fantastic night of creation?"

"Mud?" inquired Hornbeck, one eye shut.

"Associate producer of Hasurai Productions! Editor, cutter, director even—maybe. A ten-year contract! Escalations. Privileges. Stock buy-ins. Percentages. Okay now. Ready, Sam, with the pencil? Willis. What did you *do?*"

"I—" said Willis Hornbeck, "don't remember."

Aaron laughed lightly. "*Sure* you remember."

"I was drunk. Then I got scared sober. I'm sober now. I don't remember."

Aaron and I gave each other a look of pure animal panic. Then I saw something else on the floor and picked it up.

"Hold on. Wait," I said.

We all looked at the half-empty sherry bottle.

"Willis," said Aaron.

"Yes, sir?"

"Willis, old friend . . ."

"Yes, sir?"

"Willis," said Aaron. "I will now start this projection machine."

"Yes?"

"And you, Willis, will finish drinking whatever is in that bottle."

"Yes, sir."

"And you, Sam?"

"Sir?" said I, saluting.

"You, Sam," said Aaron, flicking the machine so a bright beam of light struck out into the quiet night theater and touched an emptiness that lay waiting for genius to paint incredible pictures on a white screen. "Sam, please shut and lock that heavy tin door."

I shut and locked the heavy tin door.

WELL, THE DRAGON danced at midnight film festivals all round the world. We tamed the Lion at Venice at the Venice Film Festival, we took first honors at the New York Film Festival and the Brasilia Special Prize at the World Film Competition. And not just with one film, no, with six! After *The Dragon Danced* there was the big smash international success of our *The Dreadful Ones*. There was *Mr. Massacre* and *Onslaught*, followed by *The Name Is Horror* and *Wattle*.

With these, the names of Aaron Stolittz and Willis Hornbeck were honey on the lips of reviewers under every flag.

How did we make five more smash hits in a row?

The same way we made the first one.

As we finished each film we grabbed Willis, rented the Samasuku Theater at twelve midnight, poured a bottle of the finest sherry down Willis's throat, handed him the film, started the projector, and locked the door.

By dawn our epic was slashed to ribbons, tossed like monster salad, gathered, respliced, glued fast with the epoxy of Willis Hornbeck's subliminal genius, and ready for release to the waiting avant-garde theaters in Calcutta and Far Rockaway. To the end of my insignificant life I shall never forget those nights with Willis shambling among his whirring, shadow-flickering machines, floundering about from midnight until dawn filled the patio of the Samasuku Theater with a gold the pure color of money.

So it went, film after film, beast after beast, while the pesos and rubles poured in, and one night Aaron and Willis grabbed their Academy Oscar for Experimental Film, and we all drove XKE Jags and lived happy ever after, yes?

No.

It was three glorious, fine, loving years high on the avant-garde hog. But . . .

One afternoon when Aaron was chortling over his bank account, in walked Willis Hornbeck to stand facing the big picture window overlooking Hasurai Productions' huge back lot. Willis shut his eyes and lamented in a quiet voice, beating his breast gently and tearing ever so tenderly at his own lapels: "I am an alcoholic. I drink. I am a terrible lush. I booze. Just name it. Rubbing alcohol? Sure. Mentholated spirits? Why not? Turpentine? Spar varnish? Hand it over. Nail-polish remover? Pure gargle. Rumdummy, mad fool, long-time-no-see-the-light-of-day Willis Hornbeck, but that's all over. The Pledge! Give me the Pledge!"

Aaron and I ran over and circled Willis, trying to get him to open his eyes.

"Willis! What's wrong?"

"Nothing's wrong. All's right." He opened his eyes. Tears dripped down his cheeks. He took our hands. "I hate to do this to you nice guys. But, last night . . ."

"Last night?" bleated Aaron.

"I joined Alcoholics Anonymous."

"You *what?*" screamed Aaron.

"Alcoholics Anonymous. I joined."

"You can't do that to me!" Aaron jumped up and down. "Don't you know you're the heart, soul, lungs, and lights of Hasurai Productions?"

"Don't think I haven't put it that way to myself," said Willis simply.

"Aren't you happy being a genius, Willie?" shrieked Aaron. "Fêted wherever you go? Internationally famed? That ain't enough, you got to be *sober*, too?"

"We're all so famous now," said Willis, "and loved and accepted, it has filled me up. I'm so full of fame there's no *room* for drink."

"*Make* room!" yelled Aaron. "*Make* room!"

"Ironic, huh?" said Willis. "Once I drank because I felt I was nobody. Now, if I quit, the whole studio falls down. I'm sorry."

"You can't break your contract!" I said.

Willis looked as if I had stabbed him.

"I wouldn't dream of breaking my word. But where does it say in plain English in the contract I got to be a drunk to work for you?"

My tiny shoulders sagged. Aaron's tiny shoulders sagged.

Willis finished gently.

"I'll go on working for you, always. But you know, and I know, sober it won't be the same."

"Willis." Aaron sank into a chair and, after a long and private agony, went on. "Just *one* night a year?"

"The Pledge, Mr. Stollitz. Not a drop, not once a year, even for dear and beloved friends."

"Holy Moses," said Aaron.

"Yeah," I said. "We're halfway across the Red Sea. And here come the waves."

When we glanced up again, Willis Hornbeck was gone.

It was indeed the twilight of the gods. We had been turned back into mice. We sat awhile, squeaking gently. Then Aaron got up and circled the liquor cabinet. He put out his hand to touch it.

"Aaron," I said. "You're not going to . . . ?"

"What?" said Aaron. "Cut and edit our next avant-garde epic, *Sweet Beds of Revenge*?" He seized and opened a bottle. He swigged. "All by myself? Yes!"

No.

The dead rocket fell out of the sky. The gods knew not only twilight but also that awful sleepless three o'clock in the morn when death improves on circumstance.

Aaron tried drinking. I tried drinking. Aaron's brother-in-law tried drinking.

But, look, none of us had the euphoric muse which once walked with Willis Hornbeck. In none of us did the small worm of intuition stir when alcohol hit our blood. Bums sober, we were bums drunk. But Willis Hornbeck drunk was almost everything the critics claimed, a wildman who blind-wrestled creativity in a snake pit, who fought an inspired alligator in a crystal tank for all to see, and sublimely won.

Oh, sure, Aaron and I bulled our way through a few more film festivals. We sank all our profits in three more epics, but you smelled the change when the titles hit the screen. Hasurai Films folded. We sold our whole package to educational TV.

Willis Hornbeck? He lives in a Monterey Park tract house, goes to Sunday school with his kids, and only occasionally is reminded of the maggot of genius buried in him when a critic from Glasgow or Paris strays by to chat for an hour, finds Willis a kindly but sober bore, and departs in haste.

Aaron and me? We got this little shoe-box studio thirty feet closer to that graveyard wall. We make little pictures and profits to match and still edit them in twenty-four reels and hit previews around greater California and Mexico, smash and grab. There are three hundred theaters within striking distance. That's three hundred projectionists. So far, we have previewed our monsters in 120 of them. And still, on warm nights like tonight, we sweat and wait and pray for things like this to happen: The phone rings. Aaron answers and yells:

"Quick! The Arcadia Barcelona Theater needs a preview. Jump!"

And down the stairs and past the graveyard we trot, our little arms full of film, always laughing, always running toward that future where somewhere another projectionist waits behind some locked projection-room door, bottle in hand, a look of unraveled genius in his red eye, a great blind worm in his soul waiting to be kissed awake.

"Wait!" I cry, as our car rockets down the freeway. "I left reel seven behind."

"It'll never be missed!" Aaron bangs the throttle. Over the roar he shouts, "Willis Hornbeck, Jr.! Oh, Willis Hornbeck the Second, wherever you are! Watch out! Sing it, Sam, to the tune of *Someday I'll Find You!*"

The

Nineteenth

IT WAS GETTING on toward dusk as I drove down Motor Avenue one late afternoon and saw the old man walking on the far side of the road picking up lost golf balls.

I braked the car so fast I almost fell against the windshield.

I let the car stand in the middle of the street for another ten seconds (there were no cars following), and then I slowly backed up (still no cars), until I could peer over into the gully by the golf course wire screen and see the old man bend to pick up another ball and put it in a small bucket he was carrying.

No, I thought. Yes, I thought. No.

But I swerved over and parked the car and sat a moment trying to decide what to do, a mystery of tears in my eyes for no reason I could figure, and at last got out, let traffic pass, and crossed the street heading south in the gully as the old man headed north.

We finally came face to face about fifty paces from where I had entered the gully.

"Hi," he said quietly, nodding.

"Hi," I said.

"Nice night," he said, glancing around at the turf and then down at his half-filled bucket of golf balls.

"Having luck?" I said.

"You can see." He hefted the bucket.

"Darn good," I said. "Can I help?"

"What?" he said, puzzled. "Look for more? Naw."

"I wouldn't mind," I said. "It'll be dark in another five minutes. We'd better find the darn things before it's too late."

"That's true," he said, regarding me curiously. "Why would you want to do that?"

"My dad used to come along here, years ago," I said. "He always found something. His income was small and sometimes he sold the balls for extra spending money."

"I'll *be*," said the old man. "I'm out here twice a week. Last week I sold enough balls and took my wife out to dinner."

"I know," I said.

"What?"

"I mean," I said. "Let's get going. There's one down there. And another by the fence. I'll get the one down there."

I walked down and found the ball and brought it back and stood holding it while the old man examined my face.

"How come you're crying?" he said.

"Am I?" I said. "Look at that. Must be the wildflowers. I'm allergic."

"Do I know you?" he said abruptly.

"Maybe." I told him my name.

"I'll be darned." He laughed quietly. "That's my name, too, my last name. I don't suppose we're related."

"I don't suppose," I said.

"Because I'd remember if we were. Related, that is. Or if we'd met before."

Lord, I thought, so this is how it is. Alzheimer's is one thing. Going away forever is another. With both you forget. Once you've passed over, I guess you don't need your memory.

The old man was watching me think. It made him uncomfortable. He took the golf ball from me and put it in his bucket. "Thanks," he said.

"There's another one," I said and ran down the slope and brought it back, wiping my eyes.

"You still come here often," I said.

"Still? Why not?" he said.

"Oh, I was just wondering," I said. "If I ever wanted to come hunting again, for the hell of it, if you were here it would make things easier."

"It sure as hell would," he agreed.

He studied my face again.

"Funny thing. I had a son once. Nice boy. But he went away. Never could figure where he went."

I know, I thought. But he didn't go away, *you* did. That's

how it must be, when you're saying goodbye, people seem to go away, when all the while it's you who are backing off, fading out, going and gone.

Now the sun was completely gone and we walked in half-darkness lit only by a single streetlamp across the way. I saw a last golf ball a few feet to the old man's left and nodded. He stepped over and picked it up.

"Well, I guess that's it," he said.

He looked me in the face. "Where to?" he said.

I churned my thoughts and said, glancing ahead, "Isn't there always a nineteenth hole on every course?"

The old man gazed ahead through the dark.

"Yeah. I mean, sure. There should be one up there."

"Can I buy you a drink?" I said.

"Nice of you," he said, his eyes clouded with uncertainty. "But I don't think—"

"Just one," I urged.

"It's late," he said. "I got to go."

"Where?" I said.

That was the wrong question. His eyes clouded even more. He had to search around for a lame answer.

"Well," he said. "You see," he added. "I think . . ."

"No, don't say. I hate being nosy."

"It's all right. Well. Got to be going."

He reached out to take my hand and suddenly seized it and held it tight, staring into my eyes.

"We *know* each other," he cried. "*Don't* we?"

"Yes," I said.

"But where from? How far back?" he said.

"A long way," I said.

He wouldn't let go of my hand, he clenched it tight as if he might fall.

"What did you say your name was?"

I said my name.

"Funny," he said, and then lowered his voice. "That's my name, too. Think. Us meeting here like this. And with the same name."

"That's the way it goes," I said.

I tried to pry my hand free but it wouldn't come. When I finally burst free I immediately shoved it back and took his hand in a similar vise.

"Next time," I said. "The nineteenth hole?"

"The nineteenth," he said. "You going to come back through here again?"

"Now that I know where you are. On certain nights. It's a good walking and finding place."

"Not many saps like me." He looked around at the empty grass path behind him. "Gets kind of lonely."

"I'll try to come more often," I said.

"You're just saying that."

"No. Honest to God."

"Honest to God is a good promise."

"The best."

"Well." Now it was his turn to pry his hand free and massage it to get the circulation back. "Here goes nothing."

And he ambled off. About ten feet along the far path he saw a final ball and picked it up. He nodded and gave it a toss.

I caught it easily and held it like a gift in my hand.

"The nineteenth," he called quietly.

"Absolutely," I called back.

And then he was gone in the darkness.

I stood there with tears running down my cheeks and felt the golf ball as I put it in my breast pocket.

I wonder, I thought, if it'll be there in the morning?

Beasts

SMITH AND CONWAY were almost finished with lunch when they somehow fell into a chat about innocence and evil.

"Ever been struck by lightning?" Smith asked.

"No," said Conway.

"You know anyone ever *was* struck by lightning?" said Smith.

"No," said Conway.

"They exist. A hundred thousand people get hit every year. A thousand or so die, their money fused in their pockets. Every man thinks he will never be hit by lightning. Each thinks himself a true Christian of multitudinous virtues."

"What has this to do with what we were discussing?" Conway asked.

"This." Smith lit a cigarette and peered into the flame.

"You refuse to see the prevalence of evil in our world, so I use the lightning simile to prove otherwise."

"What's the use of my recognizing evil if *you* won't accept good?"

"I do. But—" said Smith. "Until men know *two* things, the world will go merrily on to hell. First, we must see that in every good man lurks a reverse image of evil. Conversely, in every sinner, there is a marrow of good. Locking people into either category spells anarchy. Thinking a man good, we risk his duplicity. Thinking a man bad, we deny sanctuary. Most are sinner-saints. Schweitzer was a near-saint who bottled his imp or at least let it run on a leash. Hitler was Lucifer, but somewhere in him wasn't there a child frantic for escape? But that child in Hitler's burnt and gone. So slap on the label and bury his bones."

"You've gone the long way," said Conway. "Shorten it."

"All right." Smith laughed quietly. "You! Your facade is all stiff white wedding cake. Snow falls all year between your ears. Yet, beneath that whiteness, a dark heart beats, black hairs curl like watch springs. The Beast lives there. And until you can face it, one day it will unravel you."

Conway laughed. "Hilarious!" he cried. "Oh, God! Funny!"

"No, sad."

"I'm sorry," Conway gasped, "to insult you, but—"

"You insult yourself," said Smith. "And hurt your chances for a good life, later."

"Please!" Conway laughed. "Stop!"

Smith rose, face flushed.

"Now I've made you mad," said Conway, recovering. "Don't go."

"I'm not mad."

"You talk so, well, old-hat," said Conway.

"New things often seem dated," said Smith. "We surf and think it's bottom."

"Please," said Conway. "Your theories—"

"Discoveries!" said Smith. "I see you've learned nothing."

"Business prevents."

"And church on Sundays? Run by a preacher who hand-laundered you for heaven? Shall I do you a favor? I wonder. Open your eyes. Telephone PL8-9775."

"Why?"

"Call and listen tonight, tomorrow, the night after. Meet me here Friday."

"Friday—?"

"Call that number."

"Who'll answer?"

Smith smiled. "The Beasts."

Then he was gone.

Conway laughed, paid the bill, strolled forth in fine weather.

"PL8-9775?" He laughed. "Dial and say what? Hello, Beasts?"

HE FORGOT THE conversation, the telephone, and the number during dinner with his wife, Norma, said good night to her, and stayed up late reading murders. At midnight the phone rang.

He answered and said, "It must be *you*."

"Hell," said Smith, "you guessed."

"You want to know if I've dialed PL8-9775?"

"I know by your voice, no lightning's struck. Dial the number. Call!"

CALL, HE THOUGHT. Hell, no. I *won't* call!

At one in the morning the phone rang. Who's *that?* he wondered. The phone rang. This late? he thought. The phone rang. Who'd call *now?* The phone rang. Christ! The phone rang. He reached out. The phone rang. He clutched it. *Ring!* He held tight. *Ring!* Now he was wide awake! *Ring! Don't! Ring!* He grabbed but did not clap it to his ear. Why? He stared at it as if it were a huge insect, buzzing. *Whisper.* Clearer. *Whisper.* Very clear. *Whisper.* Click! He slammed it down. Christ! He had heard *nothing!* Something. *Whisper.*

He kicked the phone across the carpet. Jesus! he thought. Why *hit* it? Why?

He left it on the floor and went to bed.

But he could hear it buzzing, protesting. Finally he went in and slammed the receiver back into its cradle.

There. It was nothing. No. *Someone.* Smith? He switched off the light. Why did he think he heard several voices? Stupid. No!

He stared back into the parlor.

The phone was silent.

Good! he thought.

But he had heard *something*.

Something that brought a dampness to his face?

No!

He lay awake until . . .

Three in the long dark morning. The soul's midnight. When the dying shed their ghosts . . .

Hell!

He got out of bed and stalked in to stand over that damned Smith-inspired thing.

The mantel clock chimed three-fifteen. He raised the phone and heard it hum. He sat with the phone in his lap, and at last, slowly, dialed that number.

He had expected to hear a woman's voice, Smith's accomplice, yes, a woman. But only whispers.

And then a blur of voices, as if many calls had fused into a cloud of static. He hung up.

Then, flinching, he redialed and got the same sounds. An electric surf, neither men's nor women's voices, riding each other, protesting, some demanding, some pleading, some . . .

Breathing.

Breathing? He stifled the phone. Breathing? In, out. Phones, he thought, do not inhale, exhale.

Smith, he thought, you bastard.

Why?

Because of the strange quality of this breathing.

Strange?

Slowly he brought it up to his ear.

The voices moved apart, and all . . .

Breathing heavily, as if they had run a long way. Running in *place*. In place? How could these voices, male, female, old, young, jog, race, run in place, hold still but rise, fall, up, down?

Then all gave cries, shrieked, gasped, sucked in, blew out.

His cheeks burned. Sweat rained from his chin. Jesus! Dear Jesus God!

The phone fell.

The bedroom door slammed.

AT FOUR-THIRTY A.M. Norma Conway let her arm fall near his face. She touched his chin and brow.

"My God," she said. "You're sick."

He stared at the ceiling. "I'm all right," he said. "Go to sleep."

"But . . ."

"I'm fine," he said. "Unless . . ."

"Unless?"

"I can come over on your side of the bed."

"With that fever?"

"No, I guess not."

"Can I get you anything?"

"Nothing. Something."

He turned, his breath a furnace.

Everything, he thought, but did not say.

. . .

HE ATE A large breakfast. Norma stroked his brow and exhaled. "Thank God, it's gone."

"Gone?" He shoveled in the bacon and eggs.

"Your fever. I felt it across the bed. You're ravenous. How *come?*"

He stared at his empty plate.

"I'll be damned, yes," he said. "Sorry about last night."

"Oh, *that.*" Norma laughed gently. "I just didn't want you to hurt yourself. Better move. It's nine. What about the phone?"

On his way out, he stopped.

"Phone?"

"The wall socket looks broken. Shall I call the phone company?"

He stared at the phone on the floor.

"No," he said.

AT THE OFFICE, at noon, he took the crumpled note from his pocket.

"Stupid," he said.

And dialed the number.

The phone rang twice and a voice came on. "The number you have dialed is no longer in service."

"No longer in service!"

Almost instantly, a single line of type jumped up on the fax machine.

PL4-4559.

No signature, no address.

He dialed through to Smith.

"Smith, you bastard, what're you up to?"

"No good," Smith said triumphantly. "The old number's out of commission. Good for just one night. Try the new one. See you, drinks and dumb-talk, yes?"

"Bastard!" Conway yelled and hung up.

And went to the drinking, dumb-talk lunch.

"S A Y   I T ,"   S A I D Smith. " 'Smith, you s.o.b.' Sit. Your martini awaits. Put a straw in it."

Conway swayed over the luncheon table, making fists.

"Sit," said Smith.

Conway downed the martini.

"My, my, you're thirsty. Well," Smith leaned forward. "Tell Papa. Upchuck. Confess."

"No confessions!"

"Well then, what *almost* happened? Are you guilty, innocent, asking for mercy?"

"Shut up and drink your gin," said Conway.

"Thanks, I will. In celebration."

"Celebration?"

"Of the fact you now have the new number. The old one was a freebie. The new, if used, will cost fifty bucks. Tomorrow night, *another* new number, will run two hundred."

"My God, why?!"

"You'll be fascinated. Hooked. Not able to stop. Next week, eight hundred. You'll pay."

"*Will* I?!" Conway cried.

"Softly. Innocence rides free. Guilt costs. Your wife will question your bank balance."

"She won't! It won't happen!"

"Lord, you're Joan of Arc run amok. *She* heard voices, too."

"God's voices, not phone-sex whispers."

"True, but still she died. Waiter! Keep the drinks coming. Agreed?"

Conway jerked his head.

"Why so mad?" Smith asked. "We haven't started lunch and—"

"I haven't been *told* things!" Conway said.

"All right, all right. Are you ready?"

Smith drew on the tablecloth with his knife, and talked to the lines.

"Are you familiar with the storm drains under L.A., the dry tunnels that channel our rains, our floods?"

"I know them, yes."

"Uncover any manhole on any major street, step down in tunnels twenty miles long, all heading for the sea. All of a rainless year it's empty as a desert runoff. You must walk to the ocean someday with me, under the civilized world. Bored?"

"Continue," said Conway.

"Wait." Smith moistened his lips with his martini. "Imagine that every night at three A.M. the doors of every house on the block, every block in the tract, opened and shadows, men in their middle years, walked into the street and lifted the storm drain lids and stepped down into darkness, eh?—and moved toward that far sea they could not hear. But then it sounded louder and louder as they walked closer and closer with more shadows, all heading toward that surf at three in the morning, inhaling, exhaling, murmuring, sighing, and as they moved, as the fever from their faces lit the storm-drain walls, no need for lights, the fever does it, and the men find more tunnels in motion, a flood under houses, and the city asleep above, not knowing the surge of shadows yearning for a warm sea, whispering, wanting, in love with what? A crazed internet of flesh and blood."

"Internet, no. Crazed? Yes!"

"But this is *real!* Not laptop films. Hungry men, rushing, whispering, elbows knocking, shoes scuffing cement, on, on, until they find that far shore on a night with no moon and dawn a salvation a million miles off, but no one *wants* saving as they flood the shore of that hot sea and stand, trembling, eyes wild, by the thousands, watching volcanic waves burn the shore."

"What," said Conway, "are they *doing* there?"

"Doing? They swim that roaring furnace, that suction, to drown, inhale, exhale out, far out. You heard it last night. So you had to come. The hairs all over your body jumped. Your mouth eats cold steel, gasps flames, right?"

"No!"

"Liar!"

"No," said Conway. "What are those voices?"

"Homeless libidos, love-starved wannabees."

"*What* love is starved, *what* do they wannabe?"

"Together." Smith stirred his drink with his little finger. "To be *wildly* together."

"How?"

"By its sound, can't you *guess?* To be part of that lost soul circuit. To throw themselves in that sea of lust. Ever read Thoreau? He said most men lead lives of quiet desperation."

"Sad."

"True. Ours is the sad, desperate channel that brims Venice with unclean floods of driven men. Remember that comic strip *Desperate Ambrose?* The world swarms with men wanting, not getting, sleepless night Ambroses. Desperate. My God. Body says this, mind that. Men say yes, women *no!* Were you ever fourteen?"

"For a few years, yes."

"*Touché!* You discovered wild hot flesh, but it was years before you touched someone else's arm, elbow, mouth. How long?"

"Six years."

"Forever! Alone twenty thousand nights. Loving mirrors. Wrestling pillows. Damnation! Use the new number. Come back tomorrow."

"You've told me *nothing!*"

"*Everything.* Act! If you cancel now, to rejoin listening again costs six hundred!"

"Based on *what!?*"

"On the heavy breathing that made you trash your phone. The Bell Company reported the repairs."

"How could you know *that?*"

"No comment."

"Smith?"

Smith waited, smiling.

"Are you," said Conway, "God's Angel, or his dark son?"

"Yes," said Smith, and left.

CONWAY TELEPHONED NORMA to have the phone canceled.

"Why, for God's sake?" said Norma.

"Get the phone out. Out!"

"Madness," she said, and hung up.

He arrived home at five. Norma toured him through the house.

"Hold on," he protested, "the phone's still in the library and—"

He glanced toward their bedroom.

"They've put a new phone in there!"

"They said you insisted. Did you change the order from take *out* to put *in?*"

"My God, no," he said and walked over to stand by the new device. "Why would I do that?"

AT BEDTIME HE pulled both phones' jacks, slapped his pillow, lay down, and shut his eyes.

At three in the morning the phones rang and kept ringing. Norma's put the jacks back in the wall, he thought.

Finally, Norma stirred. "God, *I'll* do it!" She sat up.

"No!" he cried.

"What?"

"No, me!" he shouted.

"Calm down."

"I'm calm!" He seized the phone, which rang and rang as he carried it on its long cord to the other phone, which still rang and rang. He stood motionless. The bedroom door opened wider.

"Well, what are you waiting for?" Norma said.

Ignoring her, he bent to touch and then take the phone but only hold it away. The phone whispered.

At last Norma said: "So? Private calls? Is that some male-menopausal bimbo?"

"No," he said. "It is not a floozie-bubblehead-camp-follower bimbo!"

The list was so headlong that Norma laughed and shut the door.

No lie, he thought. No bimbo, floozie, bubblehead . . . It's—he hesitated, *what?* Cloud-cuckoo-land, a sinking love-boat of lost women, crazed bachelors, dry heaves, plea-bargaining, salmon migrations upstream to nowhere! What?

"Well," he said at last and went to open the bedroom door and study the cold white arctic wilderness of bed and its snowblinding empty sheets.

There was a faint rattling behind the bathroom door. The sound of aspirin shaken out as a faucet filled a glass.

He stood by the glacier bed where the floe moved never, and shivered.

The bathroom light went off. He turned and went away.

He sat quietly for an hour and then dialed the new number. No answer. And then . . .

A whisper so vast, so loud, it might comb the dead to wakening. The whispers panted from one line, two, four, ten dozen voices erupting, fused.

And it was the sound of all the girls and women he had always wanted but never had, and it was the sound of all the women he had wanted and had never wanted again, their whispers, their cries, their laughter, their mocking laughter.

And it was the sound of a sea moving in on a shore, but not the tidal floe beyond the trembling surf but a flood of flesh striking other flesh, bodies rising to fall, rising to fall and fall again with vast murmurs, incredible whispers falling, rising, until the whole volcanic mix exploded into downfalls into mindless dark. An entire population of field gymnasts rushed to leap hurdles, shouting, to drop in surfs of bodies to whine ascramble, to clutch at limbs, to writhe in midnight calisthenics, explorations, arrivals, departures clutched to teeter-totters of ascension and decline, breakaway trapeze actors who reached, seized, held, and let you plunge to strike catchers on a wild field of grabbing, rejecting arms, legs, torsos in full chorus! Orchestras of hands snatched up to grip, hug, mold. Hurricanes of cries stormed in need, dislodged their holds, then fell in rains of cooling sheets to night calms. All was silence at last except a kind of sigh that dogs might sense, and admire with barks.

Then, a *buzz*. "Deposit cash!"

"Smith, you son of a bitch," Conway said.

"That's me. Well?"

"What in hell are these voices!?"

"Aliens, neighbors, high-class Party Liners, like when we were small-town kids and our randy neighbors broadcast their pillow talks."

"Why is everyone calling at once?!"

"They're cowards, nervous Nellies, afraid of ravenous insatiables. Long-distance sumo wrestling, kick-boxing, mattress turning, top back row Elite Theater Saturday nights, drive-ins, motors killed, cars jouncing to pig squeals, weight-lifter grunts, raped canaries."

Conway was silent.

"Cat got your tongue? You a party pooper?"

"Is that a *party?*"

"Yes! Where they say what they *want* to say, hidden, old maid in Vermont, wino in Reno, Vancouver priest, altar boy Miami, stripper in Providence, college president Kankakee."

Conway was silent.

"Still there? Hate facts? Damn reality? Pay nothing! Hang up!"

Silence.

"Goodbye! Cut off, damn me, jump in bed, harass the wife! Still there? Still hot-flash wild-love delicatessen curious? Temperature a hundred and two? I'll count to three. Then triple cash for this midnight matinee. One, two . . ."

Conway bit his lip.

"You're hooked!" Smith brayed. "Got a mirror? Look!"

Conway stared at the mirror on the wall. A strange mad

pink face, slick with sweat, eyes fired, burned there. The phone voice barked!

"See? Bright cheeks. Sweat! Jaw clenched. Eyes like July Fourth!"

Conway exhaled.

"Is that a *yes!?*" cried Smith. "Last chance. Hang up or a Johnstown Flood of volcanic Krakatoa lava burns your bed. Yes? No? *Gotcha!*"

Conway at last said: "*Dozens* of people on-line?"

"Thousands! Once the word spread, mobs joined, the more mobs the higher the rates. Mobs didn't drive rates down but up. Whoever ran this late-night bender figured it was special, why not lift all the money boats in the same used bathwaters? Lots of sleepless hungers, plenty of walking wounded, much nameless dark-meat game. You *never* know who's talking. That lady, woman, girl squealing with delight, is she your old-maid schoolmarm, your sad aunt who while the old man sleeps punches Dial-A-Ride? Or your loving dad, loving the Night Family more? The Night Family, all night each night, screaming, snorting, thrashing, drained at dawn coughing hairballs with each unseen mattress-jump. Listen up! Ten thousand raw bods, Freud-crippled Christians, devoured by hello-goodbye panthers, ocelots, raw-tongued lions. Kill, kill me with love, they shout, yell, cry, please, thanks. You *there?*"

"Here," whispered Conway. "Do they ever meet?"

"Never. *Sometimes.*"

"Where?"

"The bait must home where the carnivores roam, right? They don't *want* to meet. The wires suffice for nightmare fevers, their barks so high just hyena laptop lapdogs hear. Listen."

A bedlam choir drowned in static. Yes, yes. More! Oh, yes, yes. More!

"Like them apples?" Smith cut in. "Fresh off Eden's tree. Sold by the Snake. Midnight park rentals. You will not be driven forth! Drop coins for virtual garden beds."

"Stop!" said Conway.

"Stop? Taffy-pulling your ravenous groin? Lunch, *mañana?* If you can creep or crawl to weep thanks to this sinner friend?"

"Kill you," said Conway.

"I'll duck faster than you shoot. Jump back on line. Be a torn party favor. *Ciao!*"

Click! He was gone. The storm of fevers poured in, firing his brain. More heavy breathing. He glanced up.

The wall was lit by the wild fire in his cheeks.

He let the phone fall to lie gasping unspeakable raw things as he staggered toward bed, the flames in his face lighting the floor.

He lay down with whispers and clenched his eyelids and in a moment of sleeping dream heard, far off, the clang of a metal storm drain manhole lid, lifted and slid. He blinked and jerked his head to stare across into the outer room.

Where Norma stood, the telephone thrust to her ear, eyes shut in pain as her color melted and she swayed, breathless, listening, listening.

He lifted up to call but in that instant she seized the cord and, eyes still shut, yanked the whispers out of the wall.

Sleepwalking, she glided toward the bathroom door. With no light he heard her shake and spill the aspirin bottle. The tablets rained in the toilet. The bottle fell to the floor. She flushed three times and turning, walked to stand by the bed for a moment, then lift the blanket and climb in.

After a long moment, he felt her hand touch his elbow. After another moment she whispered. *Whispered!*

"You awake?"

He nodded in the dark.

"Well," she whispered. "Now."

He waited.

"Come over," she whispered, "on *my* side of the bed."

Autumn Afternoon

"IT'S A VERY sad time of year to be cleaning out the attic," said Miss Elizabeth Simmons. "I don't like October. I don't like the way the trees get empty. And the sky always looks like the sun has bleached it out." She stood hesitantly at the bottom of the attic stairs, her gray head moving from side to side, her pale gray eyes uncertain. "But no matter what you do, here comes October," she said. "So tear September off the calendar!"

"Can I have September?" Juliet, the small niece with the soft brown hair, held the torn calendar month in her hands.

"I don't know what you'll do with it," said Miss Elizabeth Simmons.

"It isn't really over, it'll never be over." The little girl held the paper up. "I know what happened on every day of it."

"It was over before it began." Miss Elizabeth Simmons

puckered her lips and her gray eyes grew remote. "I don't remember a thing that happened."

"On Monday I roller-skated at Chessman Park, on Tuesday I had chocolate cake at Patricia Ann's, on Wednesday I got eighty-nine in spelling at school." Juliet put the calendar in her blouse. "That was this week. Last week I caught crayfish in the creek, swung on a vine, hurt my hand on a nail, and fell off a fence. That takes me up until last Friday."

"Well, it's good somebody's doing something," said Elizabeth Simmons.

"And I'll remember today," said Juliet. "Because it was the day the oak leaves started to turn all red and yellow."

"You just run and play," said the old woman. "I've got this job to do in the attic."

She was breathing hard when she climbed into the musty garret. "I meant to do this last spring," she murmured. "And here it is coming on winter and I don't want to go through all that snow thinking about this load of stuff up here." She peered about in the attic gloom, saw the huge brown trunks, the spiderwebs, the old newspapers. There was a smell of ancient wooden beams.

She opened a dirty window that looked out on the apple trees far below. The scent of autumn came in, cool and sharp.

"Look out below!" cried Miss Elizabeth Simmons, and began heaving old magazines and yellow newspapers down into the yard. "Lots better than lugging it downstairs," she gasped, shoving armloads of junk out the window.

Old wire-framed dressmaker's dummies fell careening down, pursued by silent parrot cages and riffling encyclopedias. A faint dust rose in the air and her heart went giddy so she had to find her way over to sit on a trunk, laughing breathlessly at her own inadequacy.

"My lands! Good grief!" she cried. "How it does pile up. What's this?"

She seized a box of clippings, cutouts, and obituaries, dumped them out on the trunk top, and pawed through. There were three neat small bundles of old calendar pages clipped together.

"Some more of Juliet's nonsense," she sniffed. "Honestly, that child! Calendars, calendars, saving calendars."

She picked up one page and it said OCTOBER 1887. Across its front were exclamation marks, red lines under certain days, and childish scribbles: "This was a special day!" or "A wonderful sunset!"

She turned the calendar page over with suddenly stiffening fingers. In the dim light her head bent down and her tired eyes squinted to read what was written on the back: "Elizabeth Simmons, aged ten, grammar school, low fifth."

She turned the faded pages in her cold hands and stared. She examined the dates, the years, the exclamation marks and red circles around each extraordinary time. Slowly her brows drew together. Then her eyes turned blank. Silently she lay back where she sat on the trunk, her eyes gazing out at the autumn sky. Her hands dropped away, leaving the calendar pages yellowed and faded in her lap.

July 8, 1889, with a red circle around it. What had happened that day?

August 28, 1892; a blue exclamation point. Why? Days, months, and years of marks and circles, on and on!

She closed her eyes. Her breathing came swiftly in and out of her mouth. Below on the parched autumn lawn, Juliet ran, singing.

Miss Elizabeth Simmons roused herself after a time, and moved slowly to the window. For a long while she looked down at Juliet playing among the red and yellow trees. Then she cleared her throat and called, "Juliet!"

"Oh, Aunt Elizabeth, you look so funny up there in the attic!"

"Juliet. Juliet, I want you to do me a favor."

"What?"

"Darling, I want you to throw away that nasty old piece of calendar you're saving."

"Why?" Juliet blinked up at her.

"Because, dear, I don't want you saving them anymore," said the old woman. "It'll just make you feel bad later."

"When later? And how? My gosh!" Juliet shouted. "I've got to keep every week, every month! There's so much happening I never want to forget."

Miss Elizabeth gazed down and the small round face peered up through the apple tree branches. Finally, Miss Elizabeth sighed. "All right." She looked away. She tossed the box down through the autumn air to thump on the ground. "I guess I can't stop you collecting if you must."

"Oh, thank you, Auntie, thanks!" Juliet pressed her hand to her shirt pocket where the entire month of September was stashed. "I'll never ever forget a day like today. I'll always remember, always!"

Miss Elizabeth looked down through the autumn branches that stirred in the quiet wind. "Of course you will, child," she said at last. "Of course you will."

Where All Is Emptiness There Is Room to Move

THE JEEP CAME down an empty road into an empty town beside a shoreline that was empty and a vast bay dotted with half-sunken ships stretched as far as one could see. Along the shore was a dockyard in which stood silent buildings with broken windows and huge prehistoric-looking lifters and movers, frozen somewhere back in time. For now the iron limbs and pincers and chains shook in the wind and dropped rust on the empty dock timbers where no rats ran and no cats pursued.

There was an emptiness to the entire scene that caused the young driver to slow his Jeep and gaze about at the motionless machinery and the shoreline on which not one wave arrived nor another followed.

The sky was empty, too, for with no surf or creatures within the surf to be seized, the gulls had long since sailed north of this silence, the tombstone buildings, and the dead ironworks.

The very silence of the place braked the Jeep still more so that it seemed underwater, drifting across a plaza where a population had left at dawn without disturbing the air or promising return.

"My God," the young man in the Jeep whispered. "It's really dead."

The Jeep stopped at last in front of a building on which a sign read GOMEZ/BAR. Some flags, with the colors of Mexico, rippled softly, the only motion.

The young driver got out of the Jeep slowly and was moving toward the bar when a tall man of some few years stepped forth, his hair a great white bush over his black scowl, the huge bulk of his body clad in the all-white of a bartender, a clean white towel draped over his left arm, a wineglass in the other hand. He stood scowling at the Jeep as if it were an affront and then lifted his scowl to the young man and slowly held out the glass.

"No one ever comes here," he said, in a deep guttural tone.

"So it seems," said the young man uneasily.

"No one has come here in sixty years."

"I can see that." The young man directed his gaze to the shoreline, the docks, the sea, and the air with no gulls.

"You did not expect to find anyone." It was a statement, not a question.

"No one," said the younger man. "But here you are."

"Why not? Since 1932 the town is my town, the harbor my harbor. This plaza mine. This, this is my place. Why? Out there in the harbor, it happened, years ago."

"The sandbar?"

"It came. It settled. Some ships did not escape. You see? They are rusting."

"Couldn't they clear the sandbar away?"

"They tried. This was Mexico's biggest port, with great dreams. They had an opera house. See the shops, the gilt and the tile. They all departed."

"So sand has more value than gold," said the young man.

"Yes. A little sand makes a great mountain."

"Does no one live here?"

"This one." The big man shrugged. "Gomez."

"Señor Gomez." The young man nodded. "James Clayton."

"James Clayton."

He motioned with the wineglass.

James Clayton turned silently to scan the plaza, the town, the flat sea.

"This then is Santo Domingo?"

"Call it what you will."

"El Silencio says more. Abandonado, the world's largest tomb. A place of ghosts."

"All of those."

"The Lonely Place. I have rarely known such loneliness. At the edge of town tears filled my eyes. I remembered an American graveyard in France years ago. I doubt ghosts, but I felt crushed. The air above the tombs took my breath. My heart almost stopped. I got out. This," he nodded, "is the same. Except, none are buried here."

"Only the Past," said Gomez.

"And the Past can't hurt you."

"It is always trying. Well."

Gomez looked as if he might empty the wineglass. James Clayton took the glass and said, "Tequila?"

"What else would a man offer?"

"No man that I know. *Gracias*."

"Let it shoot you. Put your head back—now!"

The young man did this, blushed and gasped. "I'm shot!"

"Let us kill you again."

Gomez backed into the bar. James Clayton stepped out of the sun.

Inside was a long bar, not the longest bar in the world like that one in Tijuana where ninety men could share murders, bark laughs, order fusillades, and die but to wake, eyeing their strange selves in the flyspecked mirrors. No, it was merely a bar of some seventy feet, well polished, and laid out with long stacks of newspapers from other years. Above these, glass chimes of crystal hung upside down, and against the mirrors stood squadrons of liquor, of all colors, waiting like soldiers, while beyond, filling the room, stood two dozen white-clothed tables on which lay bright cutlery and a few candles, lit though it was noon. Behind the bar now, Gomez set out another assassin's tequila, a slow or abrupt suicide, if the young man wished. The young man wished, staring at the empty tables and chairs, the shining silverware, the lit candles.

"You were expecting someone?"

"I do expect," said Gomez. "Someday they will come. God says. He has never lied."

"When was your last meal served? Excuse me," said James Clayton.

"The menu will say."

Sipping his tequila, Clayton picked up a menu and read:

"Cinco de Mayo, my God, May 1932! That was the last dinner?"

"Just so," said Gomez. "After the funeral for this dead town, the last woman left. The women had waited for the last man to leave. With the men gone there was no profit in staying. The hotel rooms across the way are full of butterfly wings, dresses for late dinners or the opera. Do you see that place across the plaza with golden gods and goddesses on top? Gilt, of course, or they would have been taken. In that opera the night before departure, Carmen sang, rolling cigars on her knee. When the music died, the town followed."

"No one left by sea?"

"Ah, no. The sandbar. There is a rail track behind the opera house. The last train left there in the night, with the singers singing on the porch of the observation car. I ran down the track after them, throwing confetti. I ran long after the porchful of half-fat beautiful ladies were lost in the jungle, then I sat on the rail and listened to the train vibrating the iron, my ear pressed down, tears running off my nose, *estupido*, but I stayed on. Late nights I still go to place my ear on the rail, shut my eyes, and listen, but the track is dumb. Just as stupid as ever, I come back to sit and drink and say to myself, *mañana*: yes. The arrival! And now, you."

"A poor arrival."

"You will do for now." Gomez leaned to touch one old, yellowed newspaper. "Señor, can you really know the year?"

Clayton smiled at the newspaper. "1932!"

"1932! A better year. How can we know that other years exist? Do planes fill the sky? Do the roads fill with tourists? Do warships stand in the harbor? I see none. Does Hitler live? His name is not yet here. Is Mussolini evil? Here he seems good. Does the Depression stay? Look! It will die by Christmas! Mr. Hoover says! So each day I unfold another paper and reread 1932. Who says otherwise?"

"Not I, Señor Gomez."

"Let us drink to that."

They drank the tequila and Clayton wiped his mouth.

"Don't you want me to tell you what's happening out beyond today?"

"No, no. My newspapers stand ready. One a day. In ten years I will arrive in 1942. In sixteen years I will reach 1948, by then it cannot wound me. Friends bring these papers twice a year, I simply stack them on the bar, pour more tequila and read your Mr. Hoover."

"Is he still alive?" Clayton smiled.

"Today he did something about foreign imports."

"Shall I tell you what happened to him?"

"I will not listen!"

"I was joking."

"Let us drink to that."

They quietly drank their drinks.

"I suppose you wonder why I came?" said Clayton at last.

Gomez shrugged. "I slept well last night."

"I like lonely places. They tell you more about life than cities. You can lift things and look under and no one watching so you feel self-conscious."

"We have a saying," said Gomez. "Where all is emptiness, there is room to move. Let us move."

And before Clayton could speak, Gomez strode quietly with his long thick legs and his great body out to the Jeep, where he stared down at the great litter of bags and their labels.

His lips spelled out the words:

"Life." He glanced at Clayton. "Even I have heard of that. In town I do not look left or right or listen to those radios in shops or the bar I know before my trip back with supplies. But I have seen that name on the big magazine. *Life?*"

Clayton nodded sheepishly.

Gomez scowled as he stared hard down at many black shiny metal objects.

"Cameras?"

Clayton nodded.

"Just lying there, open. You did not drive with them so, surely?"

"I opened them outside town," said Clayton. "To take pictures."

"Of what?" said Gomez. "Why would a young man leave

all things to come where there is nothing, *nada*, to take pictures of a graveyard? You're here to see more than this place," said Gomez.

"Why do you say that?"

"The way you slap at flies that are not there. You cannot stand quietly. You watch the sky. Señor, the sun will go down without your help. Do you have an appointment? You have a camera but have not used it. Are you waiting for something better than my tequila?"

"I . . ." said Clayton

And then it happened.

Gomez froze. He listened and turned his head toward the hills. "What's that?"

Clayton said nothing.

"Do you hear? Something?" said Gomez, and leaped to the bottom of an outside staircase that rose to the top of a low building, where he scowled off at the hills, shielding his eyes.

"On the road, there, where no cars have been in years. What?"

Clayton's face colored. He hesitated.

Gomez yelled down at him. "Your friends?"

Clayton shook his head.

"Your enemies?" said Gomez.

Clayton nodded.

"With cameras?" Gomez exclaimed.

"Yes."

"Speak up!"

"Yes!" Clayton said.

"Coming for the same reason you have come, yet have not

told me why?" Gomez cried, staring at the hills and hearing the sound of motors that rose and fell in the wind.

"I got a head start on them," said Clayton. "I—"

At which moment with a great razor of sound that cut the sky in half, a squadron of jets shrieked over Santo Domingo. From them, great clouds of white paper fell in blizzards. Gomez, with a maniac stare, swayed at the bottom of the steps.

"Wait!" he cried. "What the hell!"

Like a white dove, one of the pamphlets fell into his hands, which he dropped, repelled. Clayton stared at the litter at his feet.

"Read!" said Gomez.

Clayton hesitated. "It's in both languages," he said.

"Read!" Gomez ordered

Clayton retrieved one of the pamphlets. And the words were these:

SECOND NOTICE

THE TOWN OF SANTO DOMINGO WILL BE PHOTO-ATTACKED

SHORTLY AFTER NOON JULY 13TH. WE HAVE GOVERNMENT

ASSURANCE THAT THE TOWN IS EVACUATED. THAT

BEING SO, AT ONE FORTY-FIVE PROMPTLY, THE FILMING OF

PANCHO! BEGINS.

STERLING HUNT
DIRECTOR

"Attacked?" said Gomez, stunned. "*Pancho?* A director of films? California, a Hispanic state, dares bomb Santo Domingo? Gah!" Gomez ripped the pamphlet in half and then quarters. "There will be no attack! Manuel Ortiz Gonzales Gomez tells you this. Come back and see."

Gomez shook long after the thunders left the sky. Then he struck a glare at Clayton and lurched into action. He lumbered across the plaza with Clayton in pursuit. Inside, in the sudden midnight darkness at noon, he floundered along to the top of the bar, feeling rather than seeing, the newspapers in neat piles riffling under his clutch. He reached the far end of the bar.

"This should be it? Yes, yes?"

Clayton looked down at the stack of newspapers and bent close.

"What, what?" said Gomez.

"A month ago," said Clayton. "The first notice. If you had bothered to read the papers as they came, maybe—"

"Read, read!" cried Gomez.

"It says . . ." Clayton squinted, took the paper, held it up to the light. "July first, 1998. The government of Mexico has sold . . ."

"Sold? Sold what?"

"The town of Santo Domingo." Clayton's eyes roved along the line. "Sold the town of Santo Domingo to—"

"To who, what?"

"To Crossroads Films, Hollywood, California."

"Films!" Gomez shouted. "California?"

"Jesus." Clayton held the paper higher. "For the sum . . ."

"Name the sum!"

"Christ!" Clayton shut his eyes. "One million two hundred thousand pesos."

"One million two hundred thousand pesos? Food for chickens!"

"Chicken shit, yes."

Gomez blinked at the newspapers "Once I bought glasses in Mexico City, but they were broken. I did not buy them again. What for? With only one paper a day to read. So I stayed in my empty place, my country, free to walk that way to this, across and back, meeting no one, making it mine. And now this, this." He rattled the paper. "More words? What?"

Clayton translated. "A Hollywood film company, Crossroads, it says. They are remaking *Viva Villa,* the life of your rebel or whatever he was, this time titled just *Pancho!* Pamphlets have been dropped on Santo Domingo, making sure of what has been promised, that the town has been in the grave during the term of six American and two Mexican presidents. Rumor has it—"

"Rumor, what rumor?"

"Rumor has it," Clayton continued, his eyes moving along the stories in each paper, each day, "that Santo Domingo, long ago abandoned, is the hiding place of thieves, murderers, and escaped criminals. Drug trafficking is suspected. The government of Mexico will send an official party to investigate."

"Thieves, murderers, escaped criminals!" said Gomez, with

a great laugh, raising his arms up and then out to embrace himself. "Do I look like one who steals, kills, escapes, traffics in drugs? Where? From this plaza to the port where we throw cocaine to the fish? Where are my fields of marijuana? Lies!" Gomez crumpled one paper in his fist. "Bury this! Within a week it will grow more lies! The next paper! Read!"

Clayton read:

"Notices have been delivered. Warnings were dropped on the town on May ninth from the air. There was no life to be seen. The film company indicates that when *Pancho!* is finished they will use Santo Domingo for another film, *Earthquake*, to appear in ruins."

"I saw no papers in the air," said Gomez. "If they were dropped they fell into the sea to be read by sharks. Mexican aviators, yes. That is it!"

Sweeping the newspapers off the bar in one grand sweep, Gomez lurched out into the hot sun. Along the way he seized a rifle off the wall, found a sling of bullets. He loaded the weapon and sighted it at the plaza.

"Your camera, gringo," he said. *"¡Andale!"*

Clayton, at his Jeep, brought forth the best Leica, snapping it once at Gomez, who looked at Clayton and the Leica, laughed, and held the rifle across his chest.

"How do I look?"

"Like the dictator of a village, no, a country!"

"And now?" Gomez stood at attention and stiffened his neck. "Yes?"

"Yes!" Clayton snapped the Leica, laughing.

"Now." Gomez aimed at the sky. "Do you see the enemy arriving at, how do they say? Four o'clock?"

"Five." said Clayton, and snap!

"Now lower! Now higher!" Gomez aimed the rifle. This time he fired. The shot knocked birds off the trees in bright explosions. A family of parrots protested. Gomez fired again, commenting, "This gives you many fine shots, liar with the camera? It is all lies, yes? Those California people, liars with cameras? They could not get war to stand still. Dead, they could photograph it. Here, now, let me aim this way."

"Hold it, that's good!" said Clayton. "Don't make me laugh, I can't hold still."

"The only way to kill a man is to laugh. Now you, señor." He aimed the rifle at Clayton.

"Hey!" said Clayton.

Click. The rifle fell on emptiness. "No ammunition," said Gomez. "Have you enough pictures for your magazine? GENERAL GOMEZ IN ACTION. GOMEZ RETAKES SANTO DOMINGO. GOMEZ A MAN OF PEACE LOVES WAR!"

Click went the camera with a dull sound.

"Out of ammunition, that is, film," Clayton said.

They both reloaded, bullets and film, film and bullets, laughing.

"Why are you doing this?" said the young man.

"Soon those sons of whores will fly back so fast you will not be able to trap me, I will move as quickly. We take the fine pictures now so you can put the lies together later. Besides, I might die before they return. The heart at this moment is saying bad things, like lie down, be quiet. But I will neither sit, die, nor be quiet. Thank God the plaza is empty. It is easy to run and fire, fire and run with the jets. How much ahead of them do I fire to kill one?"

"It can't be done."

Gomez swore and spat. "How much lead? Thirty feet? Forty out in front? Fifty?"

"Fifty, maybe," said Clayton.

"Good. Watch! I will kill one."

"If you do you will get two ears and a tail!" said Clayton.

"One thing must be certain," said Gomez. "That I will never surrender and that I fought well and won the last battle even though I died. I should be buried in the middle of the ruins when the ruins come."

"Agreed," said Clayton.

"Now a final time, I will move more quickly, run, stop, aim, fire, run, stop, fire. Ready?"

"Ready."

Gomez did all this and stopped, gasping.

"Bring the tequila," he said, and Clayton brought it and they drank. "Well," he said, "that was a good war, yes, plenty of lies, but no one will know and you, the best liar, will be sure I appear in at least three editions about the Santo Domingo War and Gomez, the great! Do you swear?"

"It is sworn. But—"

"What of you now? Do you stay? Will you wait for your enemies?"

"No," said Clayton. "I have my story. They will not see

what I have seen. Gomez triumphant in the noon plaza. Gomez the hero of Santo Domingo."

"You lie in your teeth, but you have fine teeth," Gomez said. "Now, a pose with dignity." He dressed his rifle to one side and tucked his right hand within his blouse solemnly.

"Hold it." Clayton snapped his Leica.

"Now." Gomez eyed a shining path beyond the plaza. "Take me there." He slung himself into the Jeep, his rifle across his knees, and Clayton drove across the plaza. Gomez jumped out to kneel by the iron rail tracks.

"Christ!" Clayton cried. "What're you doing?"

Gomez smiled, head down to the rail. "I knew they would come this way. Not the sky, not the road, those are diversions. Here. Listen!"

Gomez smiled and pressed his ear to the burning-hot rail. "They did not fool me. Not jets or cars. The train as before! *Sí!* I can hear them!"

Clayton did not move.

"I order you, listen!" said Gomez, eyes shut.

Clayton glanced at the sky, and knelt in the dust.

"Good," Gomez murmured, and motioned with his free hand. "Do you hear?"

Clayton, his ear burnt by the noon iron, said nothing.

"Now," said Gomez quietly. "Far off, yes? But near."

Clayton heard something or nothing, he could not say.

"There. Closer now," murmured Gomez, greatly satisfied. "On time. After sixty years, *sí*. What year is that coming? What time is it, at last?"

Clayton's face agonized.

"Speak," said Gomez.

"July . . ."

He stopped.

"July what?"

"Thirteenth!"

"So it is the thirteenth. And . . . ?"

Clayton forced himself. "Nineteen . . ."

"Nineteen what, señor?"

"Ninety-eight!"

"July thirteenth, 1998. It has already arrived. It is already over. This I hear in the rail. Yes?"

Clayton's whole weight forced him to the track. It hammered, and if the blows came from the earth or sky, his heart could not tell. For it was hurrying, rushing, hurling itself in great thunders that racked his body or his chest. Eyes shut, he whispered: "July thirteenth, 1998."

"Now," said Gomez, head down, eyes tight, smiling. "Now I know what year I live in. Brave Gomez. Go, señor."

"I can't leave you here."

"I am not here," said Gomez. "Your year arrives this day in July, I cannot stop it. But Gomez is where? Cinco de Mayo, 1932, a good year! They may come, but I am hidden where they will never think to look. Go. *¡Andale!*"

Clayton stood up and looked at Gomez, whose head lay hard on the rail.

"Señor Gomez . . ."

"He has long departed. Go with God," came the voice at his feet.

"I beg you," said Clayton.

"Where all is emptiness," said Gomez's voice, "there is room to move. When you are gone, I will move swiftly."

Clayton got in his Jeep and gunned the motor and began to drift away.

"Gomez," he called quietly.

But there was just a body on the rail and much room. Seeking to hide in other years, Gomez had simply . . . moved.

Clayton drove out of town ahead of the thunders.

One-Woman
Show

"HOW IS IT?" asked Levering. "Married to a woman who is all woman?"

"Pleasant," said Mr. Thomas.

"You make it sound like a drink of water!"

Thomas glanced up at the critic, pouring black coffee. "I didn't mean . . . Ellen's wonderful, there's no denying that."

"Last night," said Levering, "Lord, what a show. On stage, off, on, off, a blaze of beauty, roses dipped in flaming alcohol. Lilies of the morning. The entire theater leant forward to catch her bouquet. It was as if someone had opened a door on a spring garden."

"Will you have coffee?" asked Mr. Thomas, the husband.

"Listen. Three or four times in life, if a man's lucky, he goes utterly mad. Music, a painting, one or two women, can send him stark staring. I'm a critic, yes, but I've never been so thoroughly hooked before."

"We'll drive to the theater in half an hour."

"Good! Do you pick her up every night?"

"Oh, yes, I absolutely must. You'll see why."

"I came here first, of course," said Levering, "to see the husband of Ellen Thomas, to see the luckiest man in the world. Is this your routine, every night in this hotel, waiting?"

"Sometimes I circle Central Park, take the subway to Greenwich, or window-shop on Fifth Avenue."

"How often do you watch her?"

"Why, I don't think I've seen her onstage for over a year."

"Her orders?"

"No, no."

"Well, perhaps you've seen the act so many times."

"Not that." Thomas lit a cigarette from the butt of his previous one.

"Well, you see her every day, that's the answer. An audience of one, you lucky dog, no need of a theater for you. I said to Atterson last night, what more could a man ask? Married to a woman so talented that onstage, in an hour's time, a pageant of femininity has passed, a French cocotte, an English tart, a Swedish seamstress, Mary Queen of Scots, Joan of Arc, Florence Nightingale, Maude Adams, the Empress of China. I think I hate you."

Mr. Thomas sat quietly.

Levering went on, "The libidinous side, the philandering side, of every man envies you. Tempted to stray? Don't change wives; let your wife change. Presto! She's a chandelier with ten dozen different blazes of light; the very walls of these rooms must color with her personalities. Why, a man could warm his hands at a flame like that for two lifetimes. Farewell, boredom!"

"My wife would be flattered to hear you."

"No, but isn't that what every husband wants, really, in his wife? The unexpected, the miraculous. We have to settle for much less than half that. We marry what we hope are kaleidoscopes, and wind up with one-faceted diamonds. Oh, they gleam all right, no denying that. But after the thousandth playing, even Beethoven's wonderful Ninth isn't exactly a pulse-jumper, is it?"

"We've been touring, Ellen and I," said the husband, finishing his pack of cigarettes and pouring a fifth cup of coffee. "Oh, some nine years now. Once a year, we vacation, for a month, in Switzerland." He smiled for the first time and lay back in his chair. "I really think you should interview us then, and not now. It's a better time."

"Nonsense. Always do things in the spell that takes me." Levering got up and put on his coat. He gave his watch hand a flourish. "Almost time, isn't it?"

"Oh, I suppose," said Thomas, rising slowly, exhaling.

"Snap into it, man! You're going to pick up Ellen Thomas!"

"Now, if only you could guarantee that." Thomas turned away and went for his hat. Coming back, he smiled faintly. "Well, how do I look? Like the proper setting for a diamond? Am I the right curtain for her to stand against?"

"Stolid, that's the word for you, stolid. Marble and granite, iron and steel. The proper contrast to something as evanescent as touching a match to some shallow cup of vaporing cologne."

"You are one for words."

"Yes, sometimes I just stand here and listen to myself. Absolutely amazing." Levering winked and clapped Thomas on the shoulder. "Shall we hire a coach, detach the horses, and pull the wife twice around the park?"

"Once would be enough. Just once."

And out they went.

Their taxi pulled up before the empty theater lobby. "We're early!" cried Levering happily. "Let's go in for the finale."

"Oh, no."

"What? Not see your wife?"

"You must excuse me."

"What an insult! On her behalf. Come into the theater or I'll flatten you with my fists!"

"Please, don't insist."

Levering seized his arm and strode off.

"We'll just see about this." He flung a door wide, steered Thomas through, muttering, "Quietly."

Ushers turned in the dimness, recognized Thomas, subsided. They stood in darkness. The stage was lit with bright spots of rose and lavender and a color like green trees in spring. There were six white Corinthian pillars stretched from wing to wing. The theater was drawn into itself; not a breath stirred in the night.

"Please, let go," Thomas whispered.

"Shh, respect, man, respect!" whispered Levering in return.

The woman—or was it women?—onstage moved from dark to light, to dark, to light again. It was indeed the grand finale. The orchestra played softly. The woman, alone, danced with shadows, starting at stage right, waltzing in a self-made dream, turning all crystal light, in prisms and flashes, hands up, face radiant, Cinderella at the ball, the grand whirl, the happy never-to-wake vision. Gone, behind a white pillar. A moment later, appearing, another woman, dancing less swiftly, but still with a lilt, not Cinderella now, but a society lady, accepting life, a trifle bored and sad, face shaped of white bone, remembering some far time while moving with an invisible man who, by her very aspect, was a stranger indeed. The music whirled her on to another pillar, another vanishing, gone! Levering pressed to the standing-room barrier, staring. The music whirled. And from the second pillar a third woman spun, sadder yet, resigned to the music, the sparks dying, her own diminishing in splendor, a town woman, a street woman now caught between this pillar and the next, flashing a fixed death smile in and through them, leaning on the air, arms wide, mouth wet and bright. Gone again! A fourth, fifth, sixth woman! The music exploding in a carnival wheel of light! A chambermaid, a waitress, and, at last, at the far side of the stage, a witch, gray, weaving a flicker of tinsel in her bosom, only the eyes, faintly alive, burning coals, as she minced about, hands clawing night air, lips pursed, a silken death about her, turning to stare back down the years, across the chasm, like a tired, drained, and ancient beast, on hind legs, life done, still dancing, for there was nothing else to do.

It couldn't end there; not with beauty flown. The old woman stopped completely, stared across the stage to that first pillar where the bright maid had begun, long years ago. Then, crying out, but making no noise, the old woman closed her eyes, and with a vast effort of will, wished herself across the stage to that shining illusion. It was such an effort of will that no one saw the old woman vanish, the stage remain empty some five seconds, and then, in an explosion of light, reappear again, gone backward in years. The maiden reborn with spring and summer grace, not touching the world but drifting through it in a downfall of blossoms and snow, the beauty spun forever around and around, as the curtain fell.

Levering was riven. "My God," he gasped. "I know it's sentimental claptrap, a garish display, but I'm trapped! God, what a woman!"

He turned to confront Thomas, who stood clutching the velvet rail, still staring at the stage, where now a spotlight appeared. Applause filled the theater. The curtain rose. The glorious top, white and tireless, still spun there, all crystal snow and winter flourished forever as the curtain slid up and down, no music, only the great storm of applause, which spun the winter shape more wildly.

Tears rolled town Thomas's face. He watched the curtain rise and fall upon the flashing ghost, and the tears continued. Levering took hold of his arm.

"Here now, here!"

The curtain at last cut the uproar. The theater was dark; the audience, stunned, walked out, holding to each other. Levering and Thomas were silent as they made their way to the exit.

They stood outside the theater, by the stage door. Inside, a buzzer rang somewhere on the empty stage. The theater was dead and silent. At the buzzer, Thomas went to the door opened it, went in. A minute later, he came out, leading, half-supporting, a small woman, in the darkness. The woman wore a dark kerchief tight about her face, she was dressed in a lumpy coat, her face was without color, and there were lines of exhaustion in the cheeks and under the eyes. She did not see Levering and almost blundered into him.

"Darling, this is Mr. Levering, the critic. Remember?"

"What a performance!" cried Levering. "Wonderful!"

She leaned against her husband, who murmured, "A warm bath, a rubdown, then to bed, and a good night's sleep. Wake you at noon."

She stared at Levering with no lipstick on her mouth, no color on her brows or cheeks or eyelids. She trembled.

She said something he did not hear, her words came in a tired rush, her eyes saw through and beyond him, in darkness. She half-hid behind her husband and he saw her mouth without paint and her eyes without color and her mouth moved and she said several things. Some other night, some other night, some other night in the future, someday, sometime, perhaps, but not tonight, not tonight, sometime in the future. He had to lean to hear her, in the dark, hollow, empty alley. How could she explain, how could she possibly explain to him, he was so patient, so kind, to come see her, to come here. And then, as with an inspiration, he couldn't see what she was about, she seized upon an excuse, an object, and thrust it at him, confusedly, almost with apology. She let go and he held it, she gazed into his face.

Then the waiting cab drew her attention, the cab summoned it with its yellow lights and comfortable cushions and its traveling darkness and promise of leave-taking. Then, leaning, helped, she was taken away by her husband. They abandoned the critic and she was finally in the cab, closeted, with its motor purring. The husband turned and looked across the distance at the critic, questioningly. There were tiny lines around the husband's eyes and mouth.

The critic nodded and waved. The husband nodded and entered the cab, shutting the door very quietly. The cab drove, with exaggerated slowness, away. It seemed to take five minutes, like a procession, to move down the dark alley.

The critic stood by the stage door and looked at her gift, her explanation.

A face towel. No more and no less. A towel.

He stood a long moment in the alley. He shook the towel a few times without looking at it. It was wet. It was absolutely soaking. He lifted it and drew a faint breath. It was rank with perspiration.

"Some other night," he said. Yes, he might come back ten dozen nights to receive the same gift, the same excuse. "Sly one, that husband, didn't warn me. Let it all happen. Well."

He folded the towel as neatly as possible and carried it in one hand, went out to hail a taxi, and let it drive him home. "Driver," he said, on the way, "what if you had a garden and weren't allowed to pick the flowers?"

The driver thought it over as he turned a corner. "Well," he said, "that'd be one hell of a thing!"

"Yes," said Levering. "You are right, driver. One hell of a thing."

But then it was late and the cab stopped and it was time to get out and pay the driver and go into his apartment house, carrying the towel quietly, in one hand.

All of these things Mr. Levering did.

The Laurel and Hardy Alpha Centauri Farewell Tour

THEY HAD BEEN dead for two hundred years.

Yet they were alive.

They could not possibly be arriving here at Alpha C. Twelve, the twelfth planet out from Alpha Sun, yet they were arriving.

No mobs occurred. A congregation assembled quietly at dawn to consecrate this miracle, a genetic game birthed in a mortuary cathedral to ferment laughter on far worlds.

The night before, there had been a twenty-four-hour film riot by these two saints that ended with joyful tears. Then twenty thousand fans streamed across Alpha Skyport to watch their special craft burn the sky and ignite their hearts.

Now all fell silent.

There followed a technological eruption of shadow shows, laser graffiti, and Egyptian smokes and mirrors as the Alpha

Lander gasped forth in a melange of dust and fire to form an incredible 1925 Model T Ford! An accordion car, and in its pleats two faces, one large, one small, two faces clutching their hats and waving wildly.

The Model T exploded and fell as the fat man and the thin leaped out to stare at the ruins. The fat man hurled his derby down and cried: "Well, here's another fine mess you got me into!" And then, "I can't take you anywhere!"

Then with storms of laughter they were run, half funeral, half coronation, into town.

"HI STAN, HELLO OLLIE," the TV news shouted.

"Since when are they alive?" said Will Grimes, my bartender.

"They aren't, they were, hell, it's complicated," I said, watching the hotel bar TV.

"They one of those late-twentieth-century medical tricks that help folks live ninety-nine years?"

"No."

"Virtual reality? Fiber optics plus wish fulfillment?"

"You're getting warm."

"DNA gene-splicing to rebirth pterodactyls unless the Supreme Court shoots the animals and downloads them back in time?"

"Well," I said. "It was . . ."

Just then, Laurel and Hardy ambled, or lurched, into the bar. Gasps all around. Ollie surveyed the scene.

"We," he announced, "desire a double demitasse of—"

"Gin," said Stanley.

"That," Ollie nodded, eyes shut.

"Are you for real?" Will Grimes said.

"We most certainly are." Hardy thumped his chest grandil-oquently.

"Don't we look real?" Stan piped.

"Hell." Will Grimes poured drinks. "But how come you're black-and-white, like those old two-reelers? No color."

"Easy as pie," Stan beamed.

Ollie cut in.

"Tut, Stanley. Sir, when we were first created, we were full color, but folks said, no! That's not Stan and Ollie! So, back to the lab to be bleached out, and sent to fall off roofs . . ."

"In glorious black and white," Stan blinked.

"Yes!" I exclaimed. "Your skin! Pure light!"

"Computer cosmetics!"

"Still," I said, "how come you're here, two centuries after your . . . demise?"

"We never died!" Stan piped.

"Thank you, Stanley! We never lived, never died. We are first cousins to the lightbulb, telephone, the Penny Arcade, wireless telegraph, vacuum tube, TV transistor, the Salk vaccine intra-embryo split atom DNA explorer, the fax, e-mail, Internet! One vast Humpty Dumpty back on the lab wall! In sum, a melee of mad scientists who did not reinvent dinosaurs but—"

"Two goofs chased by a Music Box downhill?" I said.

"Touché."

"Two mad Christmas tree salesmen utterly destroying a house?"

"That!"

"And in nightgowns saw a gorilla in a tutu waltz by their beds?"

"That's us!" piped Stan.

"But still, you're alive?" I protested.

"Born out of necessity. Have you heard of the Loneliness, sir?"

"Long ago. It was cured."

"We were the cure!" piped Laurel.

"Stanley! Another Bombay Ease, sir. To continue, there was this sickness called the Loneliness, that no one had predicted. In all the laboratory tests on the human body, figuring on the effects of zero gravity on the flow of blood, no one had questioned time, space, and distance. How would people survive far from Earth and all its root systems, its ambiences, for ten years or one hundred? Would space be hearth or asylum? Would it offer cosmic welcomes or booby hatches? No one knew.

"Well, there was a mass awakening one dark morning ninety years out from Earth. One young man started to cry and couldn't stop. Why? Earth was distant. Earth was gone, vanished, hard to imagine!

"No one had planned that. What a blow to the psychological midriff.

"The sobbing and crying spread. Weeping is infectious. Like those old laugh records played after World War I. Folks listened and laughed!

"Sorrow, too, was epidemic. The Loneliness increased. Overnight, everyone attended funerals for lost dreams. Crying was it!

"Remedies were needed. Old movies, old videos, were medicine. But those were ghost séances. All the actors in those films died before the first rocket touched Pluto. Not images but real humans were needed!

"That," said Oliver Hardy, "is how we were born. Not reborn, no, but first-class, first time only, forget our original births and deaths. We would not be a Second Coming, but a First Arrival.

"We were rushed to completion, flesh on flesh, nerve ends to neurons, ganglia to ganglia, with DNA implants, chromosomes nabbed from a Glendale crypt, a Santa Monica tomb, an epidermal speck, the merest electric breath, then *voilà!*"

"Laurel and Hardy!" I cried.

"Right!" Hardy laughed. "With our first appearance on the Moon and a vaudeville turn at Mars Stage One, the tears dried. The sobs died. People laughed!

"Not only did Stan and I cure morning and night sickness, but we made the Cal Tech Frankensteins rich because civilization, laughing, decided to continue Outward Bound to ensure the immortality of mankind! Laurel? Hardy? Encore! Forgive my immodesty."

Will laid out fresh glasses.

"Gin all around," he said. "Let's get this straight! Are you alive?"

"No."

"Were you dead?"

"Nope," said Stan.

"We," announced Hardy, "are the Impossibles!"

"Hold on," I said. "Shake my hand. See? Not impossible."

"No," Hardy said demurely. "The Universe is impossible. We are just an extension of that Universe."

"Tell him, Ollie," Stan chirped.

"Thank you, Stanley." Ollie planted his plump fingers on his chest. "When people ask do you believe in Darwin? Yes! Lamarck? Yes! The Old Testament? Yes! But how can you believe in Darwin, Lamarck, and God saying let there be light, all three!?" Oliver Hardy surveyed three plump fingers. "Because . . . nothing is proven! Darwin, Lamarck, the Old Testament, not proven! So, why not believe all three? Was the Universe created? Was there a Big Bang!? No. There was no Creation. The Universe, impossible, has always existed, billions of light-years, no start, no finish, in all directions, forever! Dear Lord, you cry. It had to commence sometime. No, I respond. It has been here forever. Impossible?! Yes. It surrounds us with its impossibility. So, pull up your socks. You are just as impossible as we are. We just seem a bit more strange because we exist in black and white!"

"I," said Will, my barman, "am flabbergasted."

"Flabbergast was the first Pope of Creation back ten billion billion billion nonexistent years. Hang that calendar on a wall where there is no wall."

"And?" I said.

"And," Oliver Hardy went on with haughty grandiosity, "the bottom line is Stan and I were never born, never died, yet here we are. What a grand resemblance, the Universe, Stanley and me!"

"That's it!" piped Stan.

At this instant, the TV beeper on the far side of the pub gave an excruciating wail and flooded its screen with color.

"Disaster update," a funeral voice said. "The Spoilers have arrived!"

"The Spoilers?" I said. "What do they spoil?"

"Us." Ollie thumped his chest.

"Why would anyone want to spoil you?"

We all stared at the TV, where a quiet mob had gathered outside our hotel and now moved into the lobby and up to the mezzanine.

The throng entered the bar with neither an outcry nor a shriek. Their eyes blazed but they waited, hoping to find the cinematic infidels, the Biblical degenerates, Christ's flesh gone sour. They had many names for the enemy but only carried these on small cards passed out by hand.

There was an instant of panic. I feared that Stan and Ollie might be torn to celluloid shreds. But . . .

Laurel and Hardy vanished.

"What the hell—" I heard Will gasp.

"Yes, what?" I scanned the empty air as the mob streamed in one side of the bar and out the other, leaving ten dozen pamphlets:

DOWN WITH DIGITAL GHOSTS.

LET THE DEAD BURY THE DEAD.

DNA LAZARUS, BE GONE!

ONLY JESUS IS SECOND COMING.

I stared at the pamphlets as the crowd, muttering with frustration, ignored the empty air and went away.

Laurel and Hardy reappeared.

"How," said Oliver Hardy, "do you like them apples?"

"Where were you?"

"Here!" Stan peeped and yanked his topknot. His face, his body, vanished, returned, disappeared, came back.

"Digital venetian blinds?" I cried.

"Almost," Stan said.

"Stanley," said Hardy. "Dear sir, when young, did you own a plastic ruler in which were imbedded dinosaur images?"

"Yes!"

"And when you shifted the ruler?"

"The dinosaurs reared, fell back . . . disappeared. My God! Is that what you are, how you work?"

"An approximation," announced Hardy. "You might say we are printed out on an atmospheric lenticular louver. Seen full on, we are in full display. Seen from the side—*voilà!*" Hardy blinked off and on, on and off.

"I'll be damned," said Will.

"So we see you full on and the mob saw you sideways?"

"Yes! We have never arrived, never departed. Never born,

we will never die. Now, as to those Spoilers. Why would they Spoil Stanley and me?"

"Why?"

"Because these Religious Avengers hate us because we claim the Universe is impossible." Ollie stirred his finger in the gin. "They say the Creator lit the fuse on the Big Bang. But seeing a Universe a billion light-years long, Stan and I are blind, so—"

"They would Spoil us." Stan wrote his name on the air with his nose and crossed the T.

"And," Ollie went on grandly, "Gene Kelly, Garbo . . ."

"Gene Kelly!" Will cried. "Garbo? Ninotchka?!"

"Garbo laughs. She'll be along."

"Are there many . . ." I stopped, embarrassed.

"Are there other Laurel and Hardys out beyond? Yes and no."

"Both?"

"Why not? Other Stans and Ollies morphing down the cosmos? What harm would a dozen of us do?"

"But, but, but," said Will.

"No buts, sir." Ollie scanned his derby as if it were a crystal ball. "With so much melancholy to be cured on so many needy worlds, there could be a dozen Stans and Ollies. Good gravy, the Lonely sickness might rise again to knock millions into grief."

"I know—" said Will.

"You do not know, sir, so I'll continue. When questioned by skeptics we deny our DNA family. We are the only black-

and-white ghosts who fall downstairs out of the Lazarus Internet."

"Like," piped Stan, "two peas in a pod!"

"Still, it is hard for me to believe—" I said.

"Do not believe, sir, know. Observe caterpillars and butterflies. Unrelated? Yet they are one. And what of Life itself, on Earth? How could dead rock, in primal sweats, hit by lightning, come alive? How could electric storms cause life to stir and know itself? Dunno, the scientists say. It just happened. Boy, some science! So, dear sirs, that's us. We happened. No beginning and no end. Half caterpillar, half moth."

"What's more . . ." whispered Stan, "Ollie and me, Ollie and I, will live forever."

"Forever?" I gasped.

"Isn't that what you always wanted, in the old days? When we did vaudeville in Dublin and London they shouted, 'Stan? Ollie? Don't die!'

"So," Stan finished, looking with moist eyes at the years ahead, "that's how it'll be. We'll come back for a last Farewell Tour. It's in our contract, year after year after year . . ." His voice was a falsetto whisper. ". . . forever."

"Forever," whispered someone.

"Or Eternity," said Ollie jauntily. "Whichever comes first."

"Where do you go next?" I said.

"There are planets in the Alpha complex, eight habitable, seven with colonial drops. Lots of Lonelies out there waiting for cheerleaders to show up and save a civilization. But there I go again."

"You," said Will quietly, "are Christs without the crucifixion. God's most dearly beloved intergalactic sons. Nazareth without tears."

"How you do go on," chirped Stan. "If we ever truly knew who we were, Ollie would be twice as pompous, me twice as dumb."

"I wouldn't say that!" cried Ollie.

"I just did," said Stan.

"Well," said Hardy, wiggling his fingers. "We must say ta-ta. The Centauri branch of the Irish orphans has a midnight feed. Stanley and I must head a Destruction Derby. Right, Stanley?"

"Do you never rest, never sleep?" I asked.

"With so much to do?"

"Ta-ta."

"Wait," I said.

I reached out to touch. Their handshakes, though black-and-white, were warm. "Toodle-oo," I said.

And they ambled, rolled with vaudeville jumps and leaps, out the door.

The rest of that night, suspended in laser beam Virtual Realities,

1. they met a gorilla on a flimsy bridge over a deep gorge.
2. their feet trapped in cement, they plunged into deep waters.
3. they heard a lunatic promise to twist their heads, tie their legs under their chins.

4. Laurel skipped over a picket fence. Hardy, jauntily
   trying the leap, knocked the fence down.

The grand finale was, of course, Oliver Hardy poised
atop a staircase holding a huge birthday cake, fully lit,
pompously certain of his dignity, taking just one misstep, not
down, but hurled out. With a terrible cry of despair, birthday cake and Ollie in slow motion soared until cake, candles,
and Ollie landed full on the dining-room table, Ollie's face
smashed in frosting, as the table crashed and cake and Ollie
hit the floor, and the chandelier and all the wall pictures
leaped and fell in the same instant so that pictures, chandelier, table, cake, and Ollie were buried under lit candles!
Then behold! The pictures leaped back onto walls, chandelier to ceiling, the cake reconstituted, and let Ollie go so that
he was thrown in reverse up to the top of the stairs, the cake
in his hands, glancing grandly over at us with a fake modest
glance which said, here I go again, but this time no fall, no
shriek! Watch!

And there he went again, in black and white, forever certain, forever slipping, forever dreading the upthrust target of
flimsy table, gullible pictures, guillotine chandelier.

Pandemoniums of Alpha Centauri applause.

"But when, when, oh when will you return?" I asked.

"Whenever you feel the greatest need," said Ollie. "When
the Affliction sets in, when the Loneliness stays. Now say the
magic words. What the traffic cop said when we didn't move
our wreck."

Stan and Ollie held on to their hats, waiting.

"Ollie," I said, "twiddle your tie."

Ollie twiddled his tie.

"Stan, pull your topknot."

Stan yanked his hair.

I took a deep breath and shouted:

"Git outta here, or I'll give you a ticket for blocking traffic!"

Leaping up, clapping their hats, elbows flying . . .

Laurel and Hardy got out of there.

The crying didn't stop till after the third Bombay gin.

Leftovers

RALPH FENTRISS PUT the phone down, scowling.

His wife, Emily, still seated at the breakfast table, glanced up from the morning newspaper and stopped sipping her coffee.

"Who was that?" she said.

"Beryl," said Ralph, still scowling.

"Beryl?"

"You know. Sam's girlfriend, mistress, almost his wife, lover, Beryl what's-her-name."

"Ah, yes," said Emily Fentriss, buttering her toast. "Beryl Veronique Glass. That's the only way I remember: with the whole name. Veronique, especially. Do you have a headache?"

Ralph Fentriss touched the scowl fixed to his forehead.

"I'll be damned," he said. "How did that get there?"

"What did Beryl Veronique Glass want, Ralph?"

"Us," he said, rubbing his brow.

"Us?" Emily abandoned her toast.

"For dinner," he added.

"Oh, my," said Emily.

"You can say that again."

"How many years has it been? Since Sam died, that is."

"Three, maybe four. Four, I guess."

"Can't we get out of it? The dinner, I mean."

"Tell me how," he said.

"Oh, my," said Emily Fentriss again.

"WHY," SAID RALPH Fentriss, seated in the restaurant, "do they keep calling me? Old flames, old friends of our daughters, former lovers, lamebrain suitors, flimsy girlfriends, friends of friends, first cousins to distant acquaintances. And now, tonight, what in hell are we doing here? Where is she?"

"If I recall correctly," said Emily Fentriss, drinking her second glass of champagne in preparation, "she was always late. And as for your first question, they call because you keep answering."

"You can't just hang up on people."

"No. Promise to call back, then don't."

"I can't do that."

"I know, and that's the cross you'll have to bear."

"You don't call back ever, do you?"

"No, and I have a better life for it. Beneath this silk bosom, no bleeding heart."

"Bleeding heart?"

"Every drunk in a bar thinks you're the Second Coming, every homeless bum thinks you're Jesus of Nazareth arrived to carpenter their souls, every prostitute thinks you're the lawyer to beg her case, every politician knows that your heart lies under your wallet and pours on the banana oil, every bartender tells you his life story instead of you telling him yours, every cop looks at your face and doesn't give you a ticket, every rabbi asks you to lecture Friday nights even though you're a fallen-away Baptist, every—"

"All right, all right," he said.

"I just ran out of gas anyway. Tell me again, who are you?"

"Winner of the Bleeding Heart Red Cross New Year's Award."

"And don't you forget it. Pipe down! Here she comes."

"Beryl Veronique!" Ralph Fentriss cried, with mock joy.

"Just Beryl will do," said the young woman, very lovely and, for now, very quiet.

"Sit down, sit down."

"I am, don't you see. Is that champagne? My God, this glass isn't big enough. What are you waiting for?"

He filled her glass till it overflowed.

She drank it down and gasped: "Please, sir, I want some more."

"This is going to be a long evening," murmured Emily Fentriss.

"Beg pardon," said Beryl Veronique Glass.

"Fill the glass, and mine, too, while you're at it."

With a death-rictus smile Ralph Fentriss refilled the glasses.

"Well, it's good we're all together again," he said.

"Not really," said Beryl Veronique Glass.

"How long has it been?"

"Four years, one month, and three days," said the young woman.

"Since last we met?"

"Since he died."

"Sam?"

"Why else would I be here? Top this, will you?"

He topped the champagne.

"Still bother you, does he? Sam, I mean."

"He never lets up."

"Even though he is long gone?"

"What has death got to do with it? I wonder, can you sue the deceased for harassment?"

"I never thought. Sam was persistent in life, and, I gather, dominates the moments even now that he's out of here. Go on." Fentriss glanced at his watch. "Why did you call us, of all people?"

"Because I have a new boyfriend."

"Good for you!"

"No, not good. We're both fingernails-on-the-edge-of-the-cliff. I reach up, he reaches down, but we've never touched. More than a year now, a year and two months, I've been seeing him but every time I see him I start crying. Sam again. Always Sam."

Ralph Fentriss took a healthy swig and dared to say:

"Might I make a suggestion? Your new friend, if, finally, you let him cover you, that should put a lid on the coffin."

"I beg your pardon?!"

"I'm saying, if you let your new friend make love to you, really cover you in the old Biblical sense, then Samuel, Sammy, Sam, will really be dead. At last," he added.

Beryl Veronique Glass stared at him for the longest moment until Ralph Fentriss glanced down at his dinner. Then she burst into tears.

"Don't," he said.

"I've got to," she said, and let the tears flow, with very little sound. When she was finished she examined her salad and said, "My God, look what I've done to my lettuce."

"It probably needed some salt anyway," he said, with a nervous smile.

"It did," she said. "He never has."

"Never has what?"

"My new friend. Never has. Covered me."

Fentriss ordered a good wine, waited for it to be opened and aired, and at last said, "It's time."

"I guess so."

"You know it is. Shut the casket and close the grave."

"Ohmigod," she wailed and the tears flowed again.

"I'm sorry," he said.

"Don't be. I needed to hear that. Is it all right?"

"Is what all right?"

"If he covers me? You were his best friends. So I'm asking your permission."

"Permission? Just go ahead!"

"No, no, I can't, don't you see. Because Sam loved you and
you loved him so much, so long, so intensely, since your lives
were so together, since you knew everything about one
another, since you went to school with him and were in business with him and, a long time ago, loved the same women
together, well, then, don't you see? You're all that Sam had as
family. I had to come tonight for the divorce."

Fentriss sank back in his chair. "My God, is that what it is
then, after all this time? Not just a separation, not just a part-
nership over, but a divorce, both legal and religious?"

"Religious is more like it. He worshiped both of you. He
worshiped me. It's hard to finally," she paused and almost
blurted, "get it over with. Sometimes at three in the morning
the phone rings. I'm afraid to answer. He might be calling to
say I love you."

"He can't do that."

"He might. I'm even afraid of answering it at breakfast, we
had some wonderful breakfasts, or lunch, the lunches were
amazing, do you remember the lunches? At the Grand Cascade
or out in the country at the Hôtellerie du Basbreau or out at
Pierrefonds in that no-more-than-a-sandwich-stand, but he
brought the best wine along and we drank it and the sandwiches tasted like manna. Or out at Avillon at the Hôtel de la
Poste, how many Hôtels de la Poste are there in France—?"

"I—" said Ralph Fentriss.

"Where they had that incredible tomato soup that Sam
helped invent with a thin crust over the top you had to break
through to get to the soup. Do you remember that day we
had three orders of soup and nothing else but three bottles of

Le Corton with it and it was lucky they had a room where we stayed the night, we couldn't have driven back to Paris, and you slept in the bathroom—"

"I didn't want to interfere—"

"And Sam said come to bed with us, just avert your gaze—"

"Good old Sam."

"And he meant it."

"Oh, yes, he did. This was before your time, Emily, my dear."

"No, it wasn't," said his wife. "It was just six years ago when Wilma was fourteen."

"Oh," he said.

"It was all right. I gave you permission to go. Nothing seemed wrong if Sam said so."

"Good old Sam. Anyway I stayed in the bathroom and more than averted my gaze, I stuffed Kleenex in my ears."

"I hope we didn't offend you."

"A few moans and yells of joy never hurt anyone." He poured more wine.

"And do you remember how Sam told the mayor of Paris to make the Eiffel Tower a different color? The nerve! And they did it. When they installed lights all over, a lovely soft orange, a warm sepia color, like the marble in most of the Parisian buildings. And he fought to keep some of those old dirty buses with the platforms in back where the young men could mob and yell at pretty girls as they crossed Paris. Sam did that."

"My God, yes, he did!"

"And don't you remember he was the one, no one else, not even the Hemingway Society, who got the *Weekly Tour* magazine to list Harry's Bar in that little alley just off L'Opéra where you could have a fine hot dog and a glass of beer, cheap, and hear the bartender remember Papa. And then, just around the corner at the Place Vendôme, Sam convinced the manager at the Hotel Ritz to reopen the Hemingway Bar, beautifully lit, all warm citrons and orange umbers, with Papa's picture and his books all around, and they served grappa, which no one much cared for but Papa liked it! And remember it was Sam who ran that contest in the *International Herald Tribune* under the headline WHO REALLY IS BURIED IN NAPOLEON'S TOMB and proved it was General Grant! And—"

"Hold on!" said Ralph Fentriss. "You'll run dry. Wet your whiskers."

She watched him pour the Le Corton.

"That was the wine we drank at Avillon!" she said, amazed.

He stared at it and blinked. "How come I ordered it?" he said.

A tear ran down her cheek.

"Do you know something?" he said.

"What?"

"I have a feeling you really loved Sam."

"Yes! And that's why you've got to help me exorcise him. Tell me some terrible things about him so I can begin to disrespect and then not like and maybe, at last, hate him and tell him to leave."

"Let me think. Try to recall something really despicable that he did, something truly inhumane. Ah. Mmmm. Ah. Well."

"And?"

"Can't think of a thing. Oh, sure, Sam was a cad and a bounder and a womanizer, all those good things. But do you know, it fit him like a new pair of spats, or a hunting cap, or the wrong color shoes to go with a dark suit. He no sooner did a terrible thing than it just melted away. Everyone said, oh that Sam, my God, that awful boy. There, did you hear? He never grew up. I haven't done much of it myself. But he made an art and occupation out of it. You caught him peeing off the roof and he shrugged and said, checking the weather for tomorrow. Found him in bed with your current love and he gave you that fourteen-year-old lad's blink and said, wanted to find out just what you see in her! Good show. Continue! And he sailed out the door. And you were so busy laughing, yes, laughing, you forgot you were in a rage? My God! Remember when he went to France for the Two Hundredth Anniversary of the French Revolution and told all his Parisian friends he had returned for their Failed Revolution? And before they could kill him he listed all their failures! The Revolution, ending with the Terror and Napoleon. The monarchy come and gone, the 1870 Paris Commune when the French fought the Hessians outside and killed each other inside the city. 1914? Failure. We had to save France. 1940, 1944? We fought and brought de Gaulle into Paris. Failure, failure, failure! And out of all these failures, said Sam, as his friends lifted their knives, what have you done? Created the most beautiful country in the world, and the most beautiful city in history: Paris. And his French friends sheathed their knives and kissed his cheeks. Sam! Sam!"

And now tears were rolling down his cheeks.

And now it was her turn to lean forward and say, "Know something? You loved him, too."

"Hell, I was jealous of his love for you. Don't tell anyone."

"My mouth is sealed," said Emily Fentriss, his wife in waiting, pouring more wine.

Beryl Veronique Glass finished her glass, dabbed at her mouth, reached over to dab his cheek, and rose.

"Thanks for the fifty-minute hour."

She started to open her purse.

"Stop that," he said. "Now, then. What are you going to do?"

"Go call my new boyfriend, I guess."

"And?"

"And ask him to do what you said. Cover me."

"And what if it doesn't work?"

"You mean if I'm still afraid of answering the phone at three in the morning?"

"That."

"Well," she said, slowly, "I mean I hate to ask . . . but . . . could we . . . have. Another. Dinner? Or if that's too time-consuming. Lunch. Or drinks?"

"Drinks," he said. "With dinner a possibility."

Her eyes brimmed.

"Get out of here," Ralph Fentriss said.

"Here I go," she said.

And kissed Ralph and his wife and went.

"Are you still here?" Ralph asked the woman at the table beside him.

"I felt as if I wasn't," said Emily Fentriss.

THERE WAS A young man, almost a boy, sitting at the bottom of their front steps. He did not move when Ralph and Emily Fentriss came up the walk. They stood and looked at him long enough for him to feel their presence and then he lifted his weary head and peered at them with uncertain well-spring eyes.

"Good Lord," said Fentriss, "can that be you, Willie Armstrong?"

Willie Armstrong shook his head. "It used to be."

"Christ, speak up. I can't hear you."

"I don't know who I am anymore," said the young man retrogressing to his previous boyhood. "Wilma won't speak to me."

"You haven't been seeing Wilma for six months."

"That's right," said Willie Armstrong, laying his head back down on his arms and speaking with a muffled cadence. "But she still won't take yes for an answer. I call her every day. She hangs up."

Fentriss mused. "Doesn't that tell you something?"

"Yeah," came the muffled response, "she won't talk." A

thought roused Willie Armstrong to lift his head. "Will you talk to me? Can I come in?"

"Willie, do you know what time it is?"

"I lost my watch. I've lost everything. I'll stay five minutes, I promise, just five."

"Willie, it's after midnight. Say what you must right here. We'll listen."

"Well . . ." Willie wiped his nose on the back of his hand. "You see . . ."

"I'll let you men gab." Emily Fentriss brushed by her husband. "Good night, Willie. Don't stay out late, Ralph. Bye."

Ralph Fentriss put out one hand to stop her but the door opened and shut and he was alone with Willie.

"Sit down, Mr. Fentriss." Willie patted the step by his side.

"If it's just five minutes, Willie, I prefer to stand."

"It might be ten, Mr. Fentriss." Willie Armstrong's voice wallowed into a blubber.

Fentriss stared at the doorstep. "I think I will sit."

He sat.

"Well," said Willie, "here's how it is. Wilma, she . . ."

RALPH FENTRISS ENTERED the bedroom dragging his coat and unraveling his tie. "I am now sober," he said.

His wife looked up from turning pages in a book.

"Just back from a funeral?"

"I promised to get Wilma to take one more call. What are you reading?"

"One of those silly romances. Just like real life."

"What are these?"

He nudged some scraps of notepaper on the bureau.

"Phone messages. I didn't look at them. Over to you."

He scanned one of them. " 'Urgent. Bosco.' Who's Bosco?"

"We never knew his last name. One of Tina's pals. Watched TV. Ate us out of house and home."

"Oh, yeah. Bosco." He touched another note. "Here's Arnie Ames. *'Immediamente pronto* or I'll kill myself.' Do you think he will?"

"Why not? He was a charmer, but never stopped talking."

"Motormouth, yeah. Here's a third. From Bud wondering what ever happened to Emily Junior. What ever did happen to Emily Junior?"

"That's the daughter who's in New York, writing soap operas. Does it come back to you now?"

"Oh, yeah, Emily Junior. Got out of town while the get was good. Boy, am I thirsty. Any beer in the icebox?"

"We junked the icebox years ago. We have a fridge now."

"Oh, yeah." He tossed the messages down. "You want to help with these panic notices? Someone's got to answer. How about a split? Fifty percent you, fifty me?"

"Oh no you don't."

"I thought marriage was sharing."

"Unh–unh." She turned back to her book and scowled. "Where was I?"

He ruffled the pile of messages, clutched them with a weary croupier's hand and lurched down the hall, passing one empty bedroom after another, Emily Junior's, Tina's, Wilma's, and reached the kitchen to fix the messages on the refrigerator door with some Mickey Mouse magnets. Opening it, he gasped with relief.

"Two beers, thank God, no, three!"

Fifteen minutes passed and the refrigerator door stayed open, its light playing over an almost happy becoming a happy man in his early forties, a can of beer in each hand.

Another minute passed and Emily Fentriss came shuffling along the hall in her bedroom scruffies, a robe over her shoulders.

She stood in the doorway for a long moment, examining her husband across the room as he peered into the refrigerator, examined various items, brought them forth, and turned them upside down to dump their contents into an open trash bag.

Some green peas in a small bowl. A half cup of corn. Some meat loaf and a slice of corned beef hash. Some cold mashed potatoes. Some boiled onions in cream.

The trash bag filled.

With her arms crossed, leaning against the doorsill, Emily Fentriss at last said, "What do you think you're doing?"

"Cleaning the icebox. The fridge."

"Throwing out perfectly good food."

"No," he said, sniffing some green onions and letting them fall. "Not perfectly good."

"What then?" she said, motionless.

He stared down into the trash bag.

"Leftovers," he said. "Yeah, that's it."

And shut the door, dousing the light.

"Leftovers," he said.

One More
for the Road

MY SECRETARY STUCK her head in my office and talked over my barricade of letters and books.

"You in there?" she called.

"You know I am, and overworked," I said. "What?"

"There's a maniac out here needs publishing and claims he has written or will write the World's Longest Novel."

"I thought Thomas Wolfe was dead," I said.

"This chap is carrying four shopping bags of what looks like kindling," Elsa said, "but there's letters and words on each chunk. 'It was a dark and stormy night,' one said. 'People were dead everywhere,' said another."

That did it. I rose behind my fortress of literature and marched to the door to peer out at the maniac. He sat across the reception area with several white bags containing lumps. I could see words in both.

"Bring him in," I heard myself say.

"You don't really—"

"I do," I said, wide awake. "Talk about Narrative Hooks!"

"Hooks?"

"The way you start a novel that's so wild your reader is hooked and plunges in. Go, Elsa."

Elsa went.

She brought the little man in, for he was a little less than five feet tall, earnestly dragging his white bags full of words. When he had placed two, he hurried out to fetch two more. Then he sat quietly amongst his collection as Elsa, rolling her eyeballs, shut the door.

"Well, Mr. . . . ?" I said.

"G. F. Follette, author of what some call Follette's Folly. Here is my amazing novel!"

He stirred the bags with his shoe.

"I'm intrigued, Mr. Folly," I said.

He ignored my slip and smiled down at his creations.

"Thanks. Most editors are busy or run off. Sir, I'm here because . . ." He paused to scan me head to foot. "I see you're my age and might recall that grand time, in the thirties, when tourists crossed the United States by car . . ." He paused to let me remember. I did. I nodded.

"This." He touched his bags full of words. "Is an old idea whose time has returned. Remember those trips, Route 66, heading west with your parents? On the way, how did you entertain yourself and bug the hell out of your folks?"

"Bug? Hell!" My mind whirled its Rolodex to three wins in a row.

"Burma Shave!" I cried, and calmed down. Editors must not enthuse; it jacks up the price. "Burma Shave," I murmured.

"Bull Durham Bull's-eye!" said Folly. "Though you didn't shave: Burma! America's highways were studded with B.S. signs, some called them, so you could chant couplets between Paducah and Potawatomi, Tonopah and Tombstone, Gila Gulch and Grass—"

"Yes, yes," I said, impatiently.

> *"Looking for a perfect shave,*
> *Buy our product, then you'll rave,*
> *Yesterday you were a slave,*
> *Free yourself with Burma Shave."*

"I remember," I cried, beaming.
"Of course you do!" said Folly.
I then recited:

> *"Bearded brute, jump from your cave.*
> *Freshen up with Burma Shave!"*

"What a memory!" Folly praised.

I stared at his mystery bags. "But what has that got to do with—"

"Glad you asked." He spilled two bags. Adjectives, nouns, and verbs scattered as he intoned: "Burma Shave, 1999. Dickens, 2000. Shakespeare, 2001."

"All of those?" I gasped. "On those small wooden signs?"

"No, not dead authors. Live ones. Me!"

He knelt and slid the phrases across the carpet.

"How would you like to publish the first and longest cross-country novel, spanning counties, circling small towns, skirting big cities, finishing in Seattle, where you never wanted to go but you had to find out how the Novel of the Century ended? And here it is! What say?"

I leaned to read the phrases that ran by my desk, ended at the wall.

"My secretary mentioned 'A Dark and Stormy Night—'?"

"Oh, that was a come-on," Folly laughed. "Narrative Hook! You know Narrative Hooks?"

I bit my tongue.

"This," he said, "is the wild true start of my magnum opus."

I read: "The world was coming to an end . . ." on the first plinth. The second read: "Alec Jones had six hours in which to save Earth!"

"Those are the eye-opener words of your vast best-seller?" I said.

"Can you do better?" he said.

"Well . . ."

"Wait!" he interrupted. "It gets wilder. Get ready to cut a deal."

He arranged more long kindling sticks until there were some sixty words underfoot, barring the door.

"You may well ask," he said, "why has this book's time come? When the Burma Shave verse was yanked like teeth from America's roads it left a vacuum, right?"

"We missed them, yes."

"Cross-country today there's little to see, cars go fast, bill-boards are verboten, so how to cope? Something small, low-profile on the soft shoulder, mainly side roads, from Maine to Missoula, Des Plaines to Denver. Plant these mini-metaphors to take root in the American psyche. Provoke TV chat news bites. Tourists, crazy, start reading in Kankakee, Kenosha, and Kansas. Find the finales in Sauk Center and Seattle. Then, sir, by God, we publish the whole bounteous batch in one Book-of-the-Month, leather-bound, to reap the travel tour storm winds. Think!"

"I'm overwhelmed, Folly!"

"As you should be. Quick, now! I must race to the next publisher, unless you sign and nail these revolutionary plac-ards to promote literacy in the dumbest continental backwa ters!"

"You think teachers will—"

"Devour them for breakfast, lunch, dinner! Menu them on computers. We skirt library lawns interstate advertising those drop-ins as intellectual water holes. Professors will beg to hammer my stakes near English I. Ad agencies will bribe entry to our far-traveling lingo, but no! My novel will race on, tossing characters and mad excursions right and left. Its time has come, sir. The old renewed. The untried tried again. So long!"

And he was on his feet, cudgeling his nouns and verbs, when I cried: "Wait!" I stared at the ample phrases. "These phrases are for starters, but . . . how does it end?"

"Fabulously! Once launched on the great road run, folks won't be able to stop. Crackerjack, pure crackerjack. Fritos; I dare you to eat just one!"

"How do I know—?"

"In God we trust, sir, and his man Folly's intuitive precognition. I'll weigh plot lines, hour by hour, day by day, from Schenectady to Saskatchewan. Even as I drive stakes and paint letters my secret self will dot the *i*s, cross the *t*s. I will know fevers like yours, eager to find what in hell waits beyond the 66 horizon, up early, down late, a tipped beehive of words sizzling in my wake. So?"

He snatched a dozen sticks and scanned them with relish.

"Hot diggety," he cried.

"That does it. Elsa!" I called.

"Sir?" Her head thrust in to scan the littered floor.

"God help me," I gasped. "Bring contracts. For books, I think, yes, books!"

And while she was bringing and Folly was signing I tugged his sleeve:

"Why me? Why here?"

"Sir," said Folly, "you have the mien of a librarian book-selling English major spelling-bee champ, lugged ten books from the adult stacks when you were twelve, came next noon for ten more!"

"How did you guess?"

"If I knew otherwise I wouldn't be making you grammarian editor of my movable feast! Now, how do we finance this Tolstoy-enhanced journey?"

"I don't doubt—"

"You must. We nudge lumberyards to donate plaques and stakes, gratis. Publicity! Lasso librarians for photo ops wielding mallets, or painting text. Boy Scouts eager to plant and pound. Expenses? Zilch to zero."

"Brilliant!"

"Yes? Grab your boxer shorts. Along the King's Highway, as 'twere, we flag blue-haired ladies' wedding, birth, and death card shops, hideouts for budding critics ripe to ride this Vesuvial eruption."

"Bingo!"

"Win every time! En route, traps laid by universities to bar our way."

"Why?"

"Hotbeds of unpublished authors, unfinished novels asleep in their desks, will leap out to advise punctuation, characterization, lively plot lines, dying falls."

"And . . . ?"

"Outskirts to inskirts, Philadelphia, Frisco, L.A. Antique car parades to plow us through the 'burbs. Classic cars flagging our rear. Governors at state lines, popping corks."

"Genius!"

"The squeal of my pig is not lost, sir. More details? you say. It will take some twenty thousand tent pegs flourishing twenty thousand demi-haiku fortune-cookie shingles, one every hundred yards on fast roads, every fifty yards on slow. There's your nutshell. Here's your contract. Here's mine. Now, ready cash?"

"Take this!"

"A bundle of U.S. Grants? Lincoln's pal! I'm off to the lumberyard paint shop. Premiere stake-driving-celebrity-mix tomorrow noon, old 66. You hammer the first peg!"

"I don't deserve—"

"Be there!"

And like a dust devil vacuuming the rug, he was gone, whistling to my ready cash, his kindling words ajolt in the hall.

Elsa stared. "What made you do that?" she cried.

"Teenage madness." I touched my ribs, elbows, and face. "There was a moment there when I felt thirteen, twelve, ten, the road whizzing by, the B.S. epithets in flight, me chanting, my brother echoing, my dad mad to drive off cliffs, and all of a sudden the land empty, the B.S. signs gone, when the state law dentists yanked and chopped words, and nothing to quote from Tularemia to Taos. When we pit-stopped full of soda pop, I watered Burma, my brother watered Shave."

"Nuts!" said Elsa.

"Yeah." I heard the echoes of the bags full of verbs fade. "But I can hardly wait, can you?" I whispered. "For that dark and stormy night?"

"If you say so," said Elsa.

NOT WITH A bang but a whimper, as the saying goes. What exploded as a Cecil B. DeMille rocket fizzled like a damp July Fourth squib.

I, of course, launched Folly's wild road-race epic, *On Our*

Way to Everywhere. I banged the first stake to fire off the longest novel since Appomattox. Subsequent chapters would be revealed via Council Bluffs and Gila Bend! Suspense promised! Sequels at a boil. Exclamation point.

First, no one cared. Soon: everyone!

Mobs of Folly travelers tidal-waved him cross-country, chanting phrases, reenacting scenes ere his dust settled. Letters poured in to get some characters shot, others promoted.

A *Chicago Times* critic chatted up a Folly interview, killed by his editor, an historian of Yeats and Pope. Route 66 regained its old prominence. Air travel fell. Bus travel soared. Gas stations mushroomed. Motels upped rates. Motor homes jam packed with greeting-card-ravenous readers snaked from Omaha to Oogalooga. There were Cliffs Notes digests of this brakeless ride from hell to high water.

And then, oblivion! Half out of Donner Pass, half into Death Valley, the literary freshet died.

The waterfall ran alkali dust.

The landscape was littered with white kindlings of nouns, verbs, and adjectives.

I was ready to ticket a plane or jump-start a road van when my office door banged wide. There stood Folly, truly defoliated, face pale, teeth clenched, two huge shopping bags in his downslung arms.

"Folly!" I cried.

"You can say that again," he replied.

"Come in, come in. My God, what's wrong?"

"You name it."

"Is that your sequel?"

"Residue," he murmured and spilled the bags wide.

Sawdust littered the floor. Thirty pounds of finely granulated sawdust.

"Tried, but couldn't finish," he said.

"Inspiration pooped out? Mind block?"

"Roadblock," he said.

He dumped what was left of one sack in a pile of shavings and pollen on my desk. I saw a flaked *g*, *t*, or *h* and one large *the* in the dust. The burden of this light stuff sank in my chair.

"Roadblock?" I bleated.

"I never figured folks might not want my bright wildflowers along the road," Folly mourned. "I had to skip acres of farms, sometimes entire counties. Sheriffs said: Move it! Ladies' social clubs claimed my opus was ipso facto flagrant delicti. Sex with tea! One hump or two! they yelled. Weed-pulling censors yanked my stakes, stole my stuff, as did plagiarists!"

"Plagiarists!?"

"Plot thieves, novel snatchers! Five-mile episodes vanished in Tulsa one night, showed next noon, Tallahassee to charm the alligators. Tallahassee sheriff pulled the snatch, now's a nova, Oprah celeb! How do I prove he stole my stuff!? Tried to snatch back my pick-up-sticks, but some book-burning tea party shot my tires. I told them to shove my shingles, hoping for slivers!"

He stopped, breathless.

"Roadkill," he whispered.

"Roadkill?" I cried.

"To top everything, Internet roadkill. Fast as I gardened my dears, Internet harvested and rebroadcast, galloping ahead, they the Roadrunner, I the Coyote trying to cut the electronic smog. Their fireworks blazed night and noon, firing my words on a billion screens, wiping clean, firing more, like Kasparov playing Big Blue. 'Computer Wins Chess Match!' they cried. Hell, with two dozen high-IQ minds stuffed in the IBM circuits? A wasps' nest of genius against a hopeless Russian. Same for me. This little bitty Hemingway dropout against the Internet storm. That's when I pulled up stakes and vamoosed.

"Well, that's it," said Folly. "Maybe you can rustle someone to finish the finale, kill the worst, bury the best. I failed. What can I say?"

"I hope you find a new job," I offered.

"As an adjunct carpenter running a sawmill? Good for Jesus, bad for me. I'll mail you some monthly checks, pay back the loan."

"What'll I do with this?" I said, my nose tickled by the fine wood pollen in the air.

"Stuff a pillow, start an ant farm."

"It was a fine long exciting terrific novel," I said.

"Yeah. I wonder how it would have ended."

"If you wake some night with the answer, call."

"Don't wait. So long."

And leaving the twin bags of granulated opus magnum, he left.

Elsa peered in. "What will you do with all that?" she said.

I sneezed once, twice, three times.

The desktop lay empty. Sawdust bloomed.

Elsa stared at the airborne opus.

"Gone with the Wind?" she said.

"No. Could be: Jack Kerouac *On the Road.*"

I blew my nose.

"Fetch the broom."

Tangerine

ONE NIGHT ABOUT a year ago I was having a late dinner, alone, in a fine restaurant, feeling good about myself and my place in the world (a nice feeling to have when you're in your seventies), when, sipping my second glass of wine, I glanced at my waiter, whose presence until now had been over my shoulder or at a distance.

It was like those moments in a movie when the film jerks in the projector and freezes a single image. I felt my breath catch.

I knew this waiter from another year. And knew that I hadn't seen him for a lifetime. My age, yet he was recognizable, so when he came forward to pour the rest of my wine I dared to speak.

"I think I know you," I said.

The waiter glanced at me and said, "No, I don't think—"

But, closer now, the same forehead, same cut of hair, ears, the chin, same weight as half a century back, so his face hadn't changed.

"Fifty-seven years ago," I said. "Before the war."

The waiter's eyes slid to the side, then back. "No, I don't believe—"

"1939," I said. "I was nineteen. You must've been the same."

"1939?" The waiter's gaze checked my eyebrows, ears, nose, and finally my mouth. "You don't look familiar."

"Well," I said. "My hair was light then, and I weighed forty pounds less, and I had no money for clothes, and I used to go downtown on Saturday nights to listen to the soap-box orators in the park. There was always a good fight."

"Pershing Square." The waiter nodded and half-smiled. "Yeah, yes. Sure. I went there once in a while. Summer of '39. Pershing Square."

"Most of us were just wandering young men, kids, lonely."

"Nineteen's lonely. You'll do anything, even listen to a lot of hot air."

"There was plenty of that." I saw I had him hooked. "There used to be a little gang, not really a gang, like today, but five or six guys got to know each other, we had no money, so we kind of wandered around town, sometimes dropped into a beer parlor. They'd ask you for your ID so all you could get was Cokes. Twenty-five cents I think it was for a Coke you could nurse for an hour and watch the crowd at the bar and the tables."

"Petrelli's." The waiter touched his mouth as if the words were a surprise. "I haven't thought of that place in years. But I don't remember being there with you," he said nervously. "What's your name?"

"You never knew. We just called each other 'hey' or 'you.' We might have made up some names. Carl or Doug or Junior. You could've been Ramón."

The waiter rolled his towel into a ball. "How did you know that? You must've heard—"

"No, it just came to me. Ramón, right?"

"Keep your voice down."

"Ramón?" I said quietly.

He nodded abruptly. "Well, it's been nice—"

He might have gone but I said, "We prowled around town, five or six of us, and one night one of the gang treated us to French Dip sandwiches down near City Hall. The young man who did it sang everywhere we went, sang and laughed, laughed and sang. What was his name?"

"Sonny," the waiter said suddenly. "Sonny. And there was a song he sang a dozen times a night that summer."

" 'Tangerine,' " I said.

"Ohmigod, what a memory!"

"Tangerine."

Johnny Mercer wrote it. Sonny sang it.

Leading us through the night, a small crowd of six or seven.

"Tangerine."

Sometimes we called him Tangerine, for that was his

favorite song the summer of that year before everyone went away to war. Tangerine was it. We never found out what his last name was nor where he lived now or where he came from. He was Friday nights late and Saturdays later, singing as he got off the streetcar like a great lady with refined manners and a look that said the world should have more flowers, but sadly did not.

Tangerine. Sonny. No name. He was tall for that year, just this side of six feet, with more skeleton and less flesh than the rest of us. He claimed that he was not thin but svelte and when he alighted in our midst one warm summer night the weather changed because he bade it to do so with a wave of a languid arm and pale fingers in which he held a long cigarette holder that he pointed at buildings, skylines, the park, or us, as he talked, or laughed. There was nothing he didn't laugh at, and after a while, fearing you might miss out, you joined his laughter. Life was pretty damned funny and you had best find that out now, rather than later.

Tangerine. Sonny. He drifted like a countess from a suddenly royal streetcar, swept through the park, gathering as he went all the lonelies, who, pulled by his gravity and grace, their eyes never off him, rarely speaking, followed.

It was as if they had been waiting all summer for something, anything, to happen. For someone to tell them where and who they were, and where to go. Taking it for granted, Sonny poised in the center of the red-bricked plaza, glanced about with disdain, and stabbed his cigarette holder toward those men shouting the virtues of Stalin or Hitler, choose one, choose none.

When Sonny arrived at the sound and fury, there were half a dozen aliens, wanderers in his wake. He did not glance back but accepted them, like a cape to be worn at this strange opera. He stood, eyes shut, listening to the shouts. His new friends did likewise, shut their eyes to accept the noise.

I was one of them.

And all of us nameless. Oh sure, there were Pete and Tom and Jim. But the giveaway was a young punk who claimed to be H. Bedford Jones. I knew he lied. I had read H. Bedford Jones's novels in *Argosy* when I was ten.

But who needed names when Sonny dubbed and redubbed us weekends? This one was "Squirt" and that one "Tad," and yet another "Elder Statesman," and someone— me—was from another world, or he led our late-night parades, calling out "cohorts" or "chums" or just "pals" and "lonely hearts."

I never found out much about those friends who were really not friends but late-night tourists from various cities. In later years I described L.A. and its eighty or ninety towns as eighty-five oranges in search of a navel. But in late 1939 there were only two places to socialize: Pershing Square, where the temperature rose from political explosions, or Hollywood, where people walked up and down in search of liaisons like ectoplasm that melted long before taking shape.

So it was with L.A. before the Second World War, when young men minus cars wandered in dead certain that by nine some fabulous woman would grab and hustle them home to deliriums.

It never happened. Which did not stop the young men the

next weekend from shouting "Tonight's the night" at their mirrors, knowing that when they turned away their glass images died. Thus a conglomerate gang gathered by instinct rather than intellect.

And there was Sonny.

His mirror was probably just as accurate as ours at showing defeat with nicely knotted ties and clean collars. But then mirrors are Rorschach tests; you can read anything in them that enhances your myopia or threatens your self-belief. Leaving on Saturday, you always checked the mirror to see if you were really there.

That being so, most Saturday nights were long and Sonny peacocked us around, buying hot dogs or Coca-Colas in bars full of strange men or stranger women. The men seemed to have broken wrists. The women had biceps. We nursed our Cokes for hours, stunned by the scene, until the managers threw us out.

"Okay," cried Sonny in the doorway, "if that's how you feel!"

"That's how I feel!" the managers replied.

"Come on, girls," said Sonny.

"I wish you wouldn't say that," I said.

"Sorry." Sonny left. "This way, chaps."

Some Saturday nights ended early. Sonny disappeared. And without Sonny the gang disintegrated. We didn't know what to talk about without him. We never knew where Sonny went but once we thought we saw him duck into a cheap hotel on Main Street with an old white-haired gentleman, but when we got there the lobby was empty. Another time we saw him on a bus that cost ten cents rather than a trolley that cost seven, standing by a tall slender colored boy. Then the trolley was gone. That did it. We said so long and rode home to addresses we never gave.

One Saturday night it rained without stopping and since most of the guys didn't have enough money to hide in the bars, they went home, which left Sonny and me staring at each other, until he said:

"Okay, Peter Pan, you ever had a real drink? Booze, hooch, scotch, wine."

"Nope."

"C'mon, it's time."

He dragged me into the nearest bar and ordered a Coke and a double Dubonnet. When it came, he slid it over. "Try this."

I sipped it and smiled. "Hey, not bad."

"Not bad, he says!"

"Reminds me of the grapes when I was nine that me and my dad crushed in a wine press with lots of sugar. Dubonnet."

"God! The child genius describes his first drink. When will you stop being Joan of Arc making the rounds?"

"No, no," I said. "I'm the blacksmith who made her armor."

"Give me that!" Sonny slugged the Dubonnet down. "Joan of Arc's blacksmith! Christ! Out!" Sonny paid and we were on the street, where he stopped and teetered on the curb, staring.

I looked to where he was looking. She was there.

A woman of, I would say, middle years, handsome rather than beautiful, with her hair neatly combed and pulled back in a bun. She should have been wearing a hat but she only stood with the rain falling on her face and running down the front of her black raincoat, her hands folded across her breast. When she saw us, one hand came up in a gesture as if she might call. Instead, she pulled back, as if alarmed that we might run.

"Dear God," Sonny whispered.

He sighed but did not nod to acknowledge her. "Wait!" He ducked back inside and came out a minute later, wiping his mouth. "One more for courage."

Still he made no sign of recognition, nor did he move to cross the street. The handsome middle-aged woman stood, dabbing at her eyes with a handkerchief.

"She knows you," I said.

"None of your business."

"But you're crying, too!"

"Am I?" He touched one eye and looked at the wetness on his fingertip. "Damn."

"She's crying, you're crying. Is someone dead?"

"A long time ago."

"She a relative?"

"No. Dumb woman. Crazy lady."

"What does she want?"

Sonny laughed, a crazy kind of broken laugh.

"Me."

"Beg pardon."

"Me. Me. Me! Don't you get it? She wanted me. Past tense. She wants me. Present tense. She will want me tomorrow and the day after. Some joke!"

"You're not so bad," I said lamely.

"Not so bad as what?"

"Not as bad as you think you are," I said, looking away.

"You don't know a damn thing about me!"

"I know that on Saturday nights if you left town the gang would break up."

"Some gang, a bunch of lonely half-starved idiot intellectuals with no guts and no future so they follow me like dogs peeing on fireplugs."

"It gives us something to do. You help do it."

"What does that make me?"

"A leader."

"A Christ-awful what?"

"Leader."

"Give me that head." He grabbed my skull and twisted my head. "Go have it examined."

"Sure we're nuts," I went on, with his fingers still clutching my skull. "But if you weren't around we'd all go home and stay. If you can lead us you can lead others, in some job, someplace. You're funny. You're an actor. You make us all feel good and you cover up how bright you really are."

"How bright am I?"

"You probably went to college and dropped out. Maybe you got in trouble at the men's gym. Right?" A silence. "Right?"

"You're pretty damn smart."

"Why did you never go back?"

"They wouldn't let me."

"What about some other schools?"

"You got to be kidding. This is 1939. There's a war coming. The army would claim I wear perfume and shave under my arms. Bang! I'm on the street! 'And stay out!' they'll say. Colleges pass the word. No fairies, please, at the bottom of our gardens."

"Don't talk that way about yourself."

"They do. Why not me?"

I glanced across the street, and the woman, seeing this, gave a small gesture and a half-smile, as if she guessed our discussion. Yes! I could almost read her lips. Tell him!

"How did that lady want you?"

"God, she proposed marriage!"

"Why didn't you say yes?"

"What is this, a police lineup? You got your lie detector on?"

"It's running. You can't lie to me."

"Why not?"

"Because you like me and I like you." I took a deep breath and went on.

"Do you mean to tell me that if you crossed the street now she would take you home and marry you?"

"More fool she."

"No, damn fool you."

Sonny wiped his eyes with the backs of his hands. "I thought you were my friend."

"I am."

"If I walked over you'd never see me again. The gang would break up. Where in hell would they go without me?"

"To hell with the gang. Get over there."

"It's too late." Sonny stepped back, watching her to see if she moved. "I'm drowning. No. I've gone down for the third time."

"No you haven't!"

"Besides, if I married her, she'd catch my cold. I haven't been warm in years."

I hesitated and said, "Do you want me to talk to her?"

"Nut, why would you do that?"

"Because I can't kick you downstairs. I don't like the way you're living."

"Then why the hell are you with me?"

I almost had an answer. "It's to fill time. I won't be here forever. I'll be gone in a year."

"You going to be a famous literary person?"

"Something like that."

He studied me for a long moment. "Son of a bitch. I really think you will."

"Then come on. I'll go over with you."

"The blind leading the blind? How come you're always right?"

"Because I just let things fall off my tongue and I'm surprised to hear me say them."

"You believe that crud?"

"I better. Or I won't have a life."

"Then get on with it. Take her home. I'm too old for her, for you, for everyone."

"How old are you?"

"Twenty-six."

"That's not old."

"Yes it is, if you're me and a thousand men behind me. I've got four more years, then I'm gone."

"You'll only be thirty."

"Wake up! No one wants a thirty-year-old fairy god-mother!"

I blurted it out:

"What's going to happen to you?"

Sonny froze in place and without looking at me, in a cold voice said, "I hate people asking what's going to happen to me!"

"I just mean, what? I'm asking as a friend."

"Let me look at you. Yes, poor sap, you really think you are my friend. Why," said Sonny, staring into the rain, "when I hit thirty, three-oh, I'll buy some rat poison."

"You wouldn't."

"Or a gun. Or maybe I'll defenestrate. Fine word, eh? It means jumping through a window. Defenestrate."

"Why would you do that?"

"Silly boy, someone like me, thirty's the end. No more. *Finis*. That old song: Nobody wants you when you're old and gray."

"Thirty's not old."

"Are you telling granny? Thirty's when you have to pay

for it, right? All the things you once had free, now you dig out the wallet and peel off the green. I'm damned if I'll shell out for what now is my divine right."

"I bet you talked like that when you were five."

"I was born talking. Only one way to stop me. Out the window!"

"But you have a whole life ahead."

"You maybe, dear chum, not this lady on the piano bar singing the blues. I've got fingerprints all over my skin. Not an inch isn't an FBI file of bounders, cads, and the criminally insane."

"I don't believe that."

"Poor naive sap." But he said it gently and chucked me under the chin. "You ever been kissed by a man?"

"Nope."

"I'm almost tempted." He loomed, then pulled back. "But I won't."

I fixed my gaze at that woman, it seemed, a mile away.

"How long have you known her?"

"Since high school. She was one of my teachers."

"Oh."

"Don't say 'Oh.' I was Teacher's Pet. She was never mine. She told me I was headed for great things. Pretty great, huh, downtown Saturday nights leading a dog pack of gutless wonders."

"Did you ever try to be great?"

"Jesus!"

"Well, did you?"

"Try what? Being artist, writer, painter, dancer?"

"You should have picked one."

"That's what she said. But I was busy at wild parties in Malibu or Laguna. She still hung on, and there she is, a whipped cur."

"She doesn't look whipped to me."

"No? Wait there."

I watched him through the bar-room window as he ordered another Dubonnet and made a phone call. When he came back out he said, "Just talked to Lorenzo di Medici. Know anything about the Medicis?"

"Venice, right? Formed the first banking systems? Friend of Botticelli. Enemy of Savonarola?"

"Sorry I asked. That was one of his great-great-grandsons, just asked me to live in his Manhattan penthouse in September. Secretarial work. A little light housekeeping. Thursdays off. Weekends on Fire Island."

"You going to accept?"

"She can't follow me there. Come on!"

Sonny walked off.

I looked at the woman across the street. Half an hour of rain had made her older.

I stepped off the curb. That did it. She turned away in a fresh downpour.

S UMMER   WAS   OVER.

Of course you can't tell in Los Angeles. No sooner do you think it's finished than it comes back full-blast for Thanksgiving, or spoils Halloween with 98 degrees instead of rain, or a strange hot Christmas morn with snow melted that never fell, and New Year's Eve a Fourth of July.

Anyway, summer was over, not because of season's change but just people going away, packing their grips, stashing photographs, ready to vanish in a war that was clearing its throat just beyond the ocean. You could tell summer was over in the voices of your lost and never quite found friends, whose names, if they had some, stuck in your throat. Nobody said goodbye or farewell, it was just so long, see you, with a deep sad sound to it. We all knew that whatever bus or trolley we took, we might never come back.

With the park empty on a final Saturday night, I walked Sonny to his streetcar. Just before it arrived, Sonny, not looking at me, said, "You coming along?"

"Where?" I said.

"To my place, silly."

"It's the first time you ever asked."

"Well, I'm asking now. Hurry up. I'm going away."

I looked at his profile, the pale flesh drawn over the hidden cheeks and nose and moonlit brow. He felt me examining him and turned his head to really look at me, like a discovery, for the first time.

"Thanks a lot." I hesitated and had to shift my gaze. "Thanks, but I don't think so, Sonny."

Sonny gasped.

"I'll be damned, rejected by a Martian!"

"Is that what I am?"

"Yes, yes," Sonny laughed. "But someday you'll marry

another Martian and raise a dozen kids for John Carter, War-lord of Mars."

I nodded weakly. "I think you're right."

"I am. Well, here goes, home to a lonely bed and off to the Medicis *mañana*. Sure you won't change your mind?"

"Thanks."

The trolley had stopped. He climbed up and looked down at me and the park and the city skyline, as if drinking it in, trying to remember it all.

"Sonny," I said, on impulse.

He fixed me with his liquid gaze.

"God bless," I murmured.

"I sure as hell hope so." And the trolley was moving with him in the open doorway, giving one last wave of his cigarette holder and an uplift of his slender chin.

"How does that song go?" he called. And the streetcar was lost in thunders. " 'Tangerine'? Johnny Mercer's song. All the rage that year. 'Tangerine,' " said my waiter back in another year, his face a blank on which memory wrote itself. "That strange guy, Sonny? Had a nice sweet soprano. God, I can hear him now. And the laughter. I think that was why we all followed him. No money, no jobs, no love life. Just Saturday nights to stay busy. So he sang and laughed and we followed. Sonny and 'Tangerine.' 'Tangerine' and Sonny."

The waiter stopped, embarrassed.

I finished my wine. "What," I said at last, "what ever happened to Tangerine?"

The waiter shook his head but then hesitated and shut his

eyes for a moment. "Hey. Hold on. Right after the war, in 1947, I bumped into one of those crazies, the old gang. He said he had heard, didn't know for a fact, probably true, Sonny had killed himself."

I wished my glass was full but it was empty.

"On his birthday?" I said.

"What?"

"Did he die on his thirtieth birthday?"

"How did you know that? Yeah. Shot himself."

"Thank God it was just a gun," I said at last.

"Beg pardon?"

"Nothing, Ramón. Nothing."

The waiter backed off to go get my bill, then paused.

"That song he was always singing. What were the words?"

I waited to see if he might still remember. But it didn't show in his face.

The music rose in my head. And all the old words, right on to the end.

"Don't ask me," I said.

With Smiles as
Wide as Summer

"HEY . . . HEY . . . wait for me!"

The call, the echo. The call, the echo, fading.

With apple-thudding bare feet, the boys of summer ran away.

William Smith kept running. Not because he could catch anyone but because he could not admit his feet were slower than his wish, his legs shorter than his goal.

Yelling, he plunged down the ravine at the heart of Green Town, seeking friendships hid in empty tree houses blowing their burlap-bag door curtains in the wind. Searching caves dug in raw earth, he found only burnt marshmallow fires. Wading the creek, even crayfish saw his shadow, smelled his need, and scuttled back in milk-sand explosions.

"All right, you guys! Someday I'll be older than you! Then, watch out!"

". . . Watch out . . ." said the bottomless tunnel under Elm Street.

Will slumped. Every summer—much running, no catching. Nowhere in all the town was there a boy who threw a shadow just his size. He was six. Half the people he knew were three, which was so far down you couldn't see it. The other half were nine, which was so far up, snow fell there all the year. Running after nines he had to worry about escaping the threes. It was a sad game at both ends. Now, seated on a rock, he wept.

"Who wants them? Not me, no sir! Not me!"

But then, a long way off in the noon heat, he heard a great commotion of games and frolics. Slowly, curiously, he stood up. Moving along the creek bank in shadow, he climbed a small hill, crawled under some bushes, and peered down.

There, in a small meadow at the center of the ravine, were nine summer boys, playing.

Circling, they knocked the echoes with their voices, plunged, rolled over, spun, jigged, shook themselves, raced off, hurtled back, leapt high, mad with summer light and heat, unable to stop just being alive.

They did not see William, so he had time to recall where he had seen each before. This one he remembered from a house on Elm, that one from a shoe shop on Maple, a third had last been seen leaning against a mailbox near the Elite Theater. Nameless, all nine of them, gloriously frisky, nutty with their games.

And, miracle of miracles, they were all his age!

"Hey!" cried Will.

The frolic ceased. The boys unscrambled. All gazed, some blinked at him. Some looked to set the panic off. Panting, they waited for Will to speak.

"May—" he asked quietly, "—may I play?"

They peered at him with their shining honey-warm molasses-brown eyes. Their smiles, the white smiles pinned to their faces, were wide as all of summer.

Will threw a stick far over the ravine.

"There!"

The boys, answering with their own sound, bolted off. Their furious romp kicked up vast sunlit clouds of dust.

One trotted back. The stick was in his smiling mouth. He laid it at Will's feet with a bow.

"Thank you," said Will.

The other boys ran, danced, waiting for a throw. Looking, Will thought, Cats are girls, I always knew that. But dogs, just look! All summer ahead, us here together, and dogs are nothing but—boys!

The boys barked. The boys smiled.

"You're my friends, right? We'll meet every day, right?"

They wagged their tails. They whined.

"Do like I say, and—bones and biscuits!"

The boys shivered.

"Biscuits and bones!"

He hurled the stick ten million miles out. The summer boys ran and he thought, No matter if they have pups, dogs are boys, no other animal in the whole world so much like me, Dad, Gramps. And suddenly he ran yipping, barking, fell on their dance-ground, pummeled their dusty earth, leapt their wet tree stumps. Then in a great yelling swoop they rocked off, all ten, toward wilderness country.

Under a wooden rail trestle, they froze.

A train like steel God in his wrath flashed over, along, above, away, unraveling, swift-shimmering, gone. His voice knocked forth a sweet dust in their bones.

They stood up on the empty tracks where a thousand tarbabies had melted to pools at noon. Their eyes cried with light. His summer friends showed their pink, loosely tied cravat tongues to each other.

Over them, a vast power-line tower hurled its flaming blue wires north and south in dazzles of solid electric insect-hum.

Climbing half up the tower, Will gasped.

The boys were gone!

Will shouted Hey! Boys retorted Bark!

They had trotted over to lave themselves in vast pools of butterfly shadow beneath a tree that had summoned them with the sound of the wind in its drowsy leaves. Legs out in all directions, stomachs pressed to earth, awash in green shade, they fired another cap-pistol roll of barks from their automatic throats.

"Charge!" Will slid down and off.

The boys unbathed themselves from shadow, tossed amber water-beads to telegraph pole with crisp salute of leg, then in a running march, saluting all along the way, they headed for the real lake.

There the boys dog-paddled out, the boys dog-paddled in through the great silence. A mystery lay on the shore in foam whispers and sky color which they waded through to lie on the fried sand, baking.

And lying there, Will guessed this was the best summer of his life. One like this might never happen again. For these summer-happy friends, yes, next summer and the one after that they would lie like this in water as cool or sun as hot. But next year Will, being older, might have new real friends to keep him home, fence him, draw him away from this fine sprawling, aimless time of no clocks, no beginning, no end, on these lonely sands with his unschooled and silently accepting friends. These boys, eternal children, would run forever on the rim of the world, as long as the world turned round. He did not see himself running with them anywhere beyond tomorrow.

But then at last, while his friends saluted trees, William rose and imitated his team with style and flourish. His name was writ in amber water on the sand.

"I feel sorry for girls." He looped the two *l*'s, made low hills of the *m*, and dotted the two *i*'s in his name.

The summer boys barked and scratched idle scatters of sand over the wet signature. Then proud as a gang of calligraphers, all ran into town, and with the sun tilted over his house, at long last he went up the porch steps and looked back at his independent volunteers, these tramp bum excursionists, who stood in a rough cluster on the lawn.

"This is my place, see? Tomorrow, more of the same!"

Will, in the door, felt the easy weight of the tennis shoes in one hand, warm-relaxed, and life slung in his other hand, no weight at all to palm, to bone, to whorl of thumb and fingers. He knew he smelled of dog. But then, they smelled of boy.

"Go on! S'long!"

An imaginary rabbit pelted by. In wild pretense, the team, a riot, a tumult, scurried off.

"Tomorrow!" cried Will.

And the day after and the day after that.

He watched their smiles, as wide as summer, shadow away under the trees.

Then, bearing his own smile as easily as the shoes in one hand, and life in the other, he took his happiness back through and into the cool dark pantry, where, picking and choosing, he gave it gifts.

Time

Intervening

VERY LATE ON this night, the old man came from his house with a flashlight in his hand and asked of the little boys the object of their frolic. The little boys gave no answer, but tumbled on in the leaves.

The old man went into his house and sat down and worried. It was three in the morning. He saw his own pale, small hands trembling on his knees. He was all joints and angles, and his face, reflected above the mantel, was no more than a pale cloud of breath exhaled upon the mirror.

The children laughed softly outside, in the leaf piles.

He switched out his flashlight quietly and sat in the dark. Why he should be bothered in any way by playing children he could not know. But it was late for them to be out, at three in the morning, playing. He was very cold.

There was a sound of a key in the door and the old man

arose to go see who could possibly be coming into his house. The front door opened and a young man entered with a young woman. They were looking at each other softly and tenderly, holding hands, and the old man stared at them and cried, "What are you doing in my house?"

The young man and the young woman replied, "What are you doing in our house? Here now, old man, get on out!" And the young man took the old man by the elbow, searched him to see if he had stolen anything, and shoved him out the door and closed and locked it.

"This is my house. You can't lock me out!" The old man beat at the door, then stood back in the dark morning air and looked up at the lights shining in the warm windows and rooms upstairs and then, with a motion of shadows, going out. The old man walked down the street and came back and still the small boys rolled in the icy morning leaves, not seeing him.

He stood before the house as he watched the lights turned on and turned off more than a few thousand times as he counted softly under his breath.

A boy of about fourteen ran up to the house, a football in his hand, and opened the door without unlocking it and went in. The door closed.

Half an hour later, with the morning wind rising, the old man saw a car pull up and a plump woman get out with a little boy three years old. As they walked across the wet lawn the woman looked at the old man and said, "Is that you, Mr. Terle?"

"Yes," said the old man automatically, for somehow he

didn't wish to frighten her. But it was a lie. He knew he was not Mr. Terle at all. Mr. Terle lived down the street.

The lights glowed on and off a thousand more times.

The children rustled softly in the leaves.

A seventeen-year-old boy bounded across the street, smelling faintly of the smudged lipstick on his cheek, almost knocked the old man down, cried, "Sorry!" and leaped up the porch steps and went in.

The old man stood there with the town lying asleep on all sides of him; the unlit windows, the breathing rooms, the stars all through the trees, liberally caught and held on winter branches, like so much snow suspended glittering on the cold air.

"That's my house; who are all those people going in and out?" the old man cried to the wrestling children.

The wind blew, shaking the empty trees.

In the year which was 1923 the house was dark. A car drove up before it; the mother stepped from the car with her son William, who was three. William looked at the dusky morning world and saw his house and as he felt his mother lead him toward the house he heard her say, "Is that you, Mr. Terle?" and in the shadows by the great wind-filled oak tree an old man stood and replied, "Yes." The door closed.

In the year which was 1934 William came running in the summer night, feeling the football cradled in his hands, feeling the murky night street pass under his running feet, along the sidewalk. He smelled, rather than saw, an old man as he ran past. Neither of them spoke. And so, on into the house.

In the year 1937 William ran with antelope boundings

across the street, a smell of lipstick on his face, a smell of someone young and fresh upon his cheeks; all thoughts of love and deep night. He almost knocked the stranger down, cried, "Sorry!" and ran to open the front door.

In the year 1947 a car stopped before the house, William relaxed, his wife beside him. He wore a fine tweed suit, it was late, he was tired, they both smelled faintly of too many drinks offered and accepted. For a moment they both heard the wind in the trees. They got out of the car and let themselves into the house with a key. An old man came from the living room and cried, "What are you doing in my house?"

"What are you doing in our house?" said William. "Here now, old man, get on out." And William, feeling faintly sick in his stomach, for there was something about the old man that made him feel cold, searched the old man and pushed him out the door and closed and locked it. From outside the old man cried, "This is my house. You can't lock me out!"

They went up to bed and turned out the lights.

In the year 1928 William and the other small boys wrestled on the lawn, waiting for the time when they would leave to watch the circus come chuffing into the pale-dawn railroad station on the blue metal tracks. In the leaves they lay and laughed and kicked and fought. An old man with a flashlight came across the lawn. "Why are you playing here on my lawn at this time of morning?" asked the old man.

"Who are you?" replied William, looking up a moment from the tangle.

The old man stood over the tumbling children a long

moment. Then he dropped his flash. "Oh, my dear boy, I know now, now I know!" He bent to touch the boy. "I am you and you are me. I love you, my dear boy, with all of my heart! Let me tell you what will happen to you in the years to come! If you knew! My name is William—so is yours! And all these people going into the house, they are William, they are you, they are me!" The old man shivered. "Oh, all the long years and time passing!"

"Go away," said the boy. "You're crazy."

"But—" said the old man.

"You're nuts! I'll call my dad!"

The old man backed off and walked away.

There was a flickering of the house lights, on and off. The boys wrestled quietly and secretly in the rustling leaves. The old man stood in shadow on the dark lawn.

Upstairs, in his bed, in the year 1947, William Latting did not sleep. He sat up, lit a cigarette, and looked out the window. His wife was awake. "What's wrong?" she asked.

"That old man," said William Latting. "I think he's still down there, under the oak tree."

"Oh, he couldn't be," she said.

William drew quietly on his cigarette and nodded. "Who are those kids?"

"What kids?"

"On the lawn there. What a helluva time of night to be messing around in the leaves!"

"Probably the Moran boys."

"Hell! At this hour? No, no."

He stood by the window, eyes shut. "You hear something?"

"What?"

"A baby crying. Somewhere . . . ?

"I don't hear anything," she said.

She lay listening. They both thought they heard running footsteps on the street, the front doorknob turn. William Latting went to the hall and looked down the stairs but saw nothing.

In the year 1937, coming in the door, William saw a man in a dressing gown at the top of the stairs, looking down, with a cigarette in his hand. "That you, Dad?" No answer. The man upstairs sighed and stepped back in darkness. William walked to the kitchen to raid the icebox.

The children wrestled in the soft, dark leaves of morning.

William Latting said, "Listen."

He and his wife listened.

"It's that old man," said William, "crying."

"Why?"

"Why does anyone cry? Maybe he's unhappy."

"If he's still there in the morning," said his wife in the dark, "call the police."

William Latting turned away from the window, put out his cigarette, and lay in bed, staring at the shadows on the ceiling that flicked off and on a thousand times, silently. "No," he said at last. "I won't call the police. Not for him."

"Why not?"

His voice almost whispered. "I wouldn't want to do that. I just couldn't."

They both lay there and faintly there was a sound of crying and the wind blew and William Latting knew that all he had to do if he wanted to watch the boys wrestling in the icy leaves of morning would be to reach out with his hand and lift the shade and look, and there they would be, far below, wrestling and wrestling, as the dawn came pale in the eastern sky.

With all his heart, soul, and blood he wanted to go out and lie in the leaves with them, and let the leaves bury him deep as he snuffed them in, eyes wet. He could go out there now . . .

Instead, he turned on his side and could not close his eyes, and could not sleep.

The Enemy
in the Wheat

THE FAMILY WAS deep in bed the night the enemy came to live in their wheat field.

It was midnight. The war had burned the land only forty miles away. Two small countries had been fighting each other for years, but now the war was almost finished, both sides saying, "Ah, let us quit this foolishness and go back to being human."

And then, in the dark midnight sky, the family heard a single missile cry out, the air around it whistling, so they sat up to clutch each other in their beds. The bomb struck with a loud *whump!* in their field of autumn wheat.

Silence.

The father sat higher and gasped to the quiet rooms, "Dear God, why didn't it explode? Listen! Tick, tick! Better it blew us all to a million pieces, but no! Tick, tick, tick!"

"I hear nothing. Lie down," said his wife. "You can search for the bomb tomorrow. It's away from the house. If it explodes it will knock a few pictures down."

"No, no, for God's sake, it'll flatten us all!" The father threw on a robe and hurried down and out into the wheat field.

He sniffed. "They say you can smell hot metal. We must find it before it cools. Oh, God, this misery!"

"A bomb, Father?" Tony, his smallest son, arrived behind him with a flashlight.

The father glared. "Why the flashlight?"

"I didn't want you to trip over the bomb."

"I can find more with my nose than with ten thousand flashlights." Before the son could back off, his flashlight was seized. "Did you hear? Bam! It must've knocked down a thousand trees."

"There's a tree standing over there, Father," said Tony.

The father rolled his eyeballs. "Go inside, you'll catch your death."

"It's a warm night."

"It's still summer," called his other children, swarming into the field.

"Stand back! If anyone gets blown to hell it'll be me!" cried the father.

The children went back in but left the kitchen door ajar.

"Shut that door!" The father orchestrated the flashlight beam wildly, as he stamped through the wheat field, sniffing.

When he strode into the house, his nightshirt was stitched

with burrs and tassels. "Are you still up?" he yelled at his family.

"Must you jump around like a mad bull, crushing the wheat?" asked his wife.

"Mad bull? Crushing?"

"Look." Tony pointed out of the door. "There are paths in the wheat where Papa ran up and down, east and west, back and forth."

"How soon will you grow up?" said the father. "And become a writer?"

IN THE GRAY dawn he was out in the wheat field plunging recklessly about, and then, tiptoeing, eyes afire, mouth open, probing with trembling hands. The wheat rustled in the soft wind as he stood in the center of this great mystery. Where? Where!

Only hunger brought him in at noon, but then, sandwich in hand, he was back searching, his face both fearful and pleased, excited and depressed, a furious charge and counter-charge evaporating his sweat, stopping to address the sky, the wheat field, or his own two hands. "Did you hear? Bang! Never in any war has a shell come near our farms! Woman! Bring me soup."

"Come in and get it," she replied.

"God, this waiting," he whispered. "Where's the crater? The shell must have buried itself. Dear God, the least breath . . . the tiniest touch of an ant or fly, thirty years from now. What a legacy for my sons. This enemy here, waiting to slaughter them in the next century! Think! The war ends. The heroes return. The years fly. And, one day, the hero aims his plow, cries 'Hup' to his horse, and. . . . Wham! Blown to bits!"

"Maybe it didn't land in our wheat field." Tony, his fingers laced atop his head, smiled a delicate smile.

"My God! Didn't you see the flash? It bleached the hills yellow!"

"The hills were yellow yesterday—"

"Like a great flying stove in the sky, it fell. I saw—"

"Our bedroom window's on the other side of the house," said Mother, arriving with a bowl of soup.

"So?" Father said. "Bam! Dead center in my field. God save us."

"We'll help you search," cried the children.

He stared at his wife. "Your offspring are mad." He gathered them like chicks with his beckoning and led them, whispering, to the edge of the field. "Listen, children. You're not to go near this field, even if it takes forty years to find that bomb. Anyway, perhaps it is timed to explode at two or four or eight. Today!" They listened for a long time to the wheat in the warm sun.

"Tick, tick, tick, tick," said Tony.

The father glared. "Go tell the neighbors. Go!"

Tony ran.

"The thing for us to do is to move out and ask a government official to come find your supposed bomb," said the mother calmly.

"Government officials? Where they walk, grain rots." The

father stiffened, eyes shut. "All right. Move to the village with Grandmama. Our neighbors will serve my meals. I will stay on, unafraid."

"I'm not afraid," said his wife.

"I shall remain, fearlessly."

"If you put it that way, I'll stay," said his wife. "As long as you keep your bomb away from the children."

"My bomb?"

"Here come the neighbors," she said, listening. "I must open the wine."

"Did I say bring wine?" He broke off to move to the door. From every direction, taking chances with their old hearts, men were hurrying on the roads and across the meadows, waving.

"Mostly men," observed the wife. "Fools!"

All morning long the neighbors, mostly men, gathered to stand courteously at the edge of the wheat, listening with great attention to this neighbor whose harvest might be terror.

"It must have been from that big gun I've heard about," said the father.

"Tall Tom," said little Tony.

The father's hands froze in the air. He blinked and swallowed slowly as color rose in his face like wine filling a glass.

"From forty miles away they shoot this great cannon," he continued.

"Tall Tom is its name," Tony smiled gently.

"Why," asked the father, "are you not in school?"

"You told us to stay home," answered Tony. "So we won't miss the terrible explosion that will kill all our cows."

"Well, then, bring more wine. The best!" The father

turned to regard his friends. "Remember, after the Great War, ten thousand farmers died bravely when they tripped on old mines, kicked ancient bombs, and went straight to hell!"

They all nodded, their faces serious but shining with light and anticipation.

"The least noise—bam!" whispered the father.

"A heartbeat even," suggested a neighbor.

"Yes, even a heartbeat."

Tony ran in. "Here's your wine!" he cried.

"Shh, in the name of God!"

"But here!" screamed Tony, holding up two bottles.

The father squinted at the labels. "No, no!" he cried. "This isn't the best!"

"Mother said," replied Tony in a sweet voice, "that second-best is first choice for good-for-nothings."

The bottle was uncorked in anger that melted in the warmth of the second-best wine as the men touched shoulders and laughed quietly.

"My wife," said the father, "is a wreck. Our children do not sleep well."

The neighbors peered at the house. In her kitchen, the mother calmly stirred soup and hummed a carefree song.

"Shut that door!" cried the father, then turned to his friends, remembering to whisper. "Now, let me tell you about this terrible bomb—"

"Enough," said Peter, his nearest neighbor. "We'll search the field."

"You mustn't," cried the father.

"But you can't leave it!"

"It will explode," said the father proudly. "I won't have my very dear, close friends blown to smithereens for me," said the father. "Besides, I have a strategy. In the end I will triumph over that killing device. But one must proceed slowly."

"Meanwhile," said Peter, "here comes Joseph with his metal detector."

The father recoiled in horror. "No, no, take it away!"

Joseph held the device up. "All I do is walk through the field and—"

"Bang!" someone said.

"Take it." Joseph offered the machine.

"No, don't rush him," said Peter. "He needs time."

"All must be done carefully," said another.

"Where's that Best Wine?" said a third.

The wine sparkled in the sunlight by the edge of the field. A cool breeze moved through the wheat and over the men, standing alert in the good warm day, shoulders bumping, elbows rubbing, voices mingling, mouths smiling, eyes bright. Among them, the father thought of all the fine mornings to come, getting up and striding to the field like a lad, gazing out at his splendid, mysterious harvest, sniffing the cool morning air, awaiting the arrival of his newfound friends for the replanning of strategies and blueprints. And each day, the voices of passing strangers calling: "Hey, I hear your farm's a graveyard!" Or: "You insured? When do you disappear? Is that bomb as big as your silo?"

"Bigger," he'd reply. "Oh friends, we shake in our beds,

we quake and wonder when in hell it will blow us to king-
dom come!"

"Sounds terrible!"

"Oh, it is, yes, it is!"

And he would smile as they circled the field, drawing little
maps, sending to town for cheese and bread as more travelers
tied their horses by the road and stood to stare.

But just when he was wine-deep in reverie and good fel-
lowship, there was a great cry.

Out in midfield stood little Tony.

"Hey, Papa!"

"Tony!" screamed the father.

Tony jumped up and down. "Boom!" He skipped and did
somersaults. "Boom!"

"Get out, child of hell. You'll be torn to bits!"

"Boom!" Tony laughed, stomping.

The other farmers blinked. "Hold on. Is there a bomb out
there? Look. Your son's not afraid."

"The boy was damaged by God," shrieked the father.
"Come out of there, idiot!"

Tony, smiling, moved from the field.

"What were you trying to do?" his father cried.

"Explode," said Tony, and walked off, hands over his mouth.

AT SUPPER ON the fourth night, Mother stood for a
long while at the window, gazing at the autumn wheat blowing in the wind.

"And you're just going to let the wheat stand there?"

"If we hire the reapers, who will pay for their coffins and candles?"

"In one more day, it will be too late for the wheat. Wine, visitors, talk, more wine." She turned calmly, went out the door, across the yard into the field.

"Come back!" he shouted.

An hour later she returned, gave him a long steady look, and said, "Tomorrow we harvest."

"But if we harvest—"

"People will not believe the bomb was ever there, yes? Well, I stomped every inch of that field and I still live. We harvest. Tomorrow."

THE FATHER DID not sleep well that night. Several times he awoke to scowl at his sleeping wife. He scowled into the next room at sleeping Tony. "That boy knows something," he muttered. "Dancing up and down. Fool!"

In bed he lay listening to the rich wheat blowing and the stars turning in the sky. What a life he'd had. If he ran to the village shouting, "My wife just had a daughter!" someone would say, "So? My wife has delivered a son." If he arrived panting to announce, "My wife has birthed a son," someone would snort: "Hell, Roberto's wife just had two sons!" If he said, "My wife is sick," someone would counter, "My wife is dead!" Nothing balanced. His wheat never had the decency to rot or his barn to collapse, while all around neighbors' silos burned and grandfathers were ruined by lightning. Thus were his friends lavishly provided conversations for a lifetime with much left over. He couldn't very well say, could he, "Remember the summer my barn didn't burn?" No!

Nor were his crops huge enough to be the objects of jealousy. They were casual, on the norm. "Neither bigger nor smaller than anyone else's. What kind of crop is that?"

But now, here he was, very happy indeed, and tomorrow another day which could be as pleasant as wine and conversation or as full of doom as the gleam of a scythe or the color of his wife's stare.

Well, well, we shall see, he thought, and shut the trap on his thoughts and snuffed out the small candle in his head.

AT SIX O'CLOCK in the morning, the explosion came.

His wife sat up and said, "It wasn't very loud."

"It almost destroyed the house!" he cried.

Smoke rose in the sky. Other men were running from great distances as he leaped out his door.

"It was here!"

"No, over there!"

"No, that way!"

They ran into and around and across the wheat.

"It's outside the fence," called Peter.

"No, idiot, inside, inside."

The children hurried up in their nightgowns.

"There," said Tony, pointing beyond the fence, "like Peter said!"

Fifty yards beyond and outside the wheat field, down by a little stream, stood a fresh, smoking crater.

Father stared bleakly for a long time.

"It's not very big," Tony observed.

"It's big," said Father.

"It's no bigger than my head," said Tony.

The neighbors ran up, shouting. Father stood with staring eyes which saw nothing. "It was bigger than a stove," he said to himself. "Anyway," he added, "this bomb was certainly not my bomb at all."

"What?!" everyone cried.

"No," said the father seriously. "My bomb landed in my field. Like a locomotive from the sky. You could see the flames, the iron wheels, the steaming whistle, and almost, the engineer waving, that's how big it was."

"But, but, that would make two shells!"

"One, two, dammit!" said Father. "They both landed at once! But mine was a monster. Not like that midget there. Besides, it's outside my property."

"Just fifty feet," said Tony.

"A million miles!"

"But it's not logical both fell at once. No other bombs have come within miles in all our lives."

"Nevertheless, the enemy is still hidden in my field of beautiful wheat."

"Papa," whispered Tony, pointing.

Everyone turned.

And there, walking quietly through the field of golden wheat, a gleaming scythe cradled in her arms, nodding to all the neighbors, was Mother. She stopped before her husband and very slowly, quietly, handed him the scythe.

.   .   .

MANY YEARS LATER, when he was drinking wine at the village inn, the father would hold up his glass and, after many sighs and exhalations, glance at some stranger from the corner of his eyes and at last speak. "Have you ever heard of the great bomb that fell in my wheat field and still lies ticking there today?" A grievous sigh. "See these gray hairs? They come from living cheek by jowl with the fiend, the devil grinning under my crops all these terrible years. See how drawn and lined is my face from never knowing when, plowing or asleep, I'll be blown to oblivion."

"Well," all the strangers would say, "why don't you just pack up and move?"

"Do I look like a coward?" the father would cry. "No, dear God, we'll stay on, plowing, sowing, reaping, living on borrowed time. And one morning you will see my name listed as a casualty of the war long finished, but which threatens and darkens my precious wheat. Yes, thanks, I will have a bit more of that wine . . ."

And with the burning of many calendars, and the children grown and gone, the father still could not tolerate Tony of the delicate face and the tiny white hands. Many times in the following years, Tony would write from London or Paris or Budapest, his face smiling his Madonna smile out of the delicate penmanship. Always, at the very end of his note, his parting salutation was one gentle word: "Boom."

Fore!

THE SUN WAS going down and in a few swift minutes it dipped below the horizon and the shadows came out from under all the trees, and one by one the golf-range practicers scabbarded their clubs, packed their golf balls, shucked their dark glasses, and headed for the parking lot. When the sun was completely gone the cars had gone with it; the lot was empty, the driving range abandoned, or almost abandoned.

Glenn Foray was checking some figures on his computer in the small office behind the tee-off point when he heard it. Once, twice, three times.

Whack, whack, whack.

Good solid blows of a club against three balls.

That was not ordinary.

Glenn Foray glanced up.

To the far left of the range, situated on the tee with an old-

fashioned niblick driver in hand and his tartan cap pulled low
on his brow, stood a now-familiar figure, a man who had been
in and out of the range for some years but now was bending
to tee three more balls as if it must be done quickly. Then he
straightened up, adjusted his club, and whack, whack, whack
again.

Glenn Foray regarded the missing sun, the empty car lot
with but two cars, his own, and this lone golfer's. He rose
from his desk and went to stand in the doorway, watching.

The routine was repeated. One, two, three. Whack, whack,
whack. The golfer was starting a third attack when Glenn
Foray arrived to his right. The man seemed not to notice and
drove the golf balls, one after another, far out on the green
fairway.

Foray watched them sail, then said,

"Evening, Mr. Gingrich. Nice go."

"Was it? Did it?" Gingrich said, having ignored where the
balls landed. "Well, yes. Sure. Evening. Quitting time?"

Foray waited as Gingrich placed three more. There was
something in the man's face and the way his arm stretched
and his knuckles clutched the missiles that stopped his agree-
ment.

"Quitting time?" he said. "Not yet."

Gingrich stared at the golf balls on the new tees. "Glad to
hear that. Just a few more?"

"Hell," said Foray quietly. "Take your time. I got some
figures to add. Be here at least another half hour."

"Good news." Gingrich had a nice backswing and follow-through. One, two, three. "I know it's not your job. But could I have, oh, say, two or three more buckets?"

"No sweat." Foray turned, went, and brought back three more fully loaded golf ball carriers. "Here you go."

"Thanks," said Gingrich, still not looking up, shoving more tees in the turf. His cheeks were flushed, his eyes hot with a kind of sporting frenzy as if he were playing against himself and not happy. His fingers, thrust down, seemed flushed with color, too. "Very kind of you," he almost shouted.

Foray waited for three more solid cracks and three high-flying white balls before he backed off.

From the office doorway he watched Gingrich attack with an even more concerted energy, blow after blow, almost as if he were striking—what?—a bad day at the office? A fellow golfer? A dishonest friend? Foray snorted at his own one, two, three hard-driven thoughts.

At his computer he tried to recall what he had been summing up, but still the solid blows came as the twilight set in and the night lamps switched on, flooding the empty fairway with light. It was late on a Sunday, the one night when the range closed early, and still the man with the angry eyes and the crimson face slammed the balls high and before they fell thrust more tees in place to empty the buckets.

By the time they were empty, Foray had carried two more full loads out, quietly, and set them down. Gingrich, seeing this as an act of friendship, nodded his thanks and continued his robot performance. One, two, three, one, two, three, one—

Foray did not move for a long while. At last he said, "Everything okay, Mr. Gingrich?"

Gingrich hit another three and then at last looked up. "What could not be okay?" he said.

And there were tears in his eyes.

Foray swallowed and could find no words until at last he said, looking at the crimsoned cheeks of the man and the fiery eyes, "As long as it's all okay, then. Okay."

Gingrich nodded abruptly and lowered his head. A few clear drops of water fell from his eyes.

Foray said, "I just figured. It'll take me another forty minutes, an hour, to finish up. You can close the joint with me."

"Fine. Damned fine," Gingrich said.

And clipped three clumps of grass and turf.

Foray felt the blows as if the club hit his midriff, they were that intense. The effect was like a film speeded up. No sooner were the balls up than they were gone. The air seemed full of white birds sailing in the night trees.

Foray kept rising to go to the doorway and stare out, taking the impacts, stunned with the progress of this lonely game.

"None of my business," he murmured, but still turned to his computer. He called up the index of frequent players: Galen, Gallager, Garnes . . . Here it was. Whack, whack, whack, in the twilight.

"Gingrich. William. 2344 Patricia Avenue, L.A. 90064. Mr. and Mrs. (Eleanor). Golf practice lessons early on. Repeat a few months ago. Steady customer." All the notes he had typed himself.

He looked out at the range and watched the man in his almost lunatic frenzy and wondered, Do I bring more buckets, yes, no? He brought more buckets. This time, Gingrich did not even glance up or nod.

Foray, like a man walking underwater, for reasons he did not quite understand, moved out toward his open-top roadster, listened to the constant knock, saw more white objects fly in a sky where the moon was slowly rising, and drove away.

What do I say? he thought. Mrs. Gingrich, come get your husband?

When he had parked in front of 2344 Patricia Avenue he looked in at the large Georgian house where some, not all, of the lights were lit. He saw shadows moving to one side in the windows. He heard distant music and dim sounds of laughter.

To hell with this, he thought. What's wrong with you? Fool!

He stepped on the gas and started to glide away but in his head he heard the chopping sounds, one, two, three, and stopped and coasted the car back near the curb. He waited a long while, chewing his lower lip, cursing, and at last got out, stood swaying, and moved up the walk. He stood before the front door for another long minute listening to the soft voices inside and the music playing low, and at last touched the doorbell with almost as much force as the lone player thrusting in the tees. Silence. He rang again. More silence. One, two, three. Three thrusts. Three bell sounds, each louder.

He stopped and waited.

At long last the door opened and a woman's face appeared.

Her hair was tousled and her face was moist with a faint perspiration. Her eyes adjusted to his face and she said, "Yes?"

"Mrs. Gingrich?" Foray said.

"Yes?" She seemed confused, and glanced swiftly over her shoulder. In a far doorway, Foray saw the shadow of a man, or what seemed the shadow of a man.

"Yes?" she said again, quickly.

He swayed in place. One, two, three. Knock, knock, knock. Crack, crack, crack. No one else heard the sounds. He wet his lips, closed his eyes, opened them, and for some reason said, "I'm Gingrich."

"What?" she said, even more confused.

"Gingrich, William," he said, louder.

"You're not my husband!" she said.

"Yes," he said. "I am."

And hauled off and struck her in the mouth with his fist. As she held her lips with both hands, falling back, he cried, "And if you come out, you'll get the same!"

The shadow in the far door did not move. Foray turned and walked back underwater to the car and drove away.

At the driving range Gingrich was still hitting the white objects, striking the blows, mechanically, downswing, strike, downswing, crack, downswing, bang!

Foray appeared nearby with a golf bag full of clubs.

Gingrich paused and looked at the bag.

"What?" he said.

Foray said, "How about one last round?"

Gingrich looked at the open fairway to his left. A wire screen door opened there to the first tee.

"This late at night?" he said.

"It's never too late," said Foray. "I'll carry the clubs."

"I'll be damned," said Gingrich.

"Not if I can help it," said Foray.

Gingrich said, "We won't be able to see."

"We will." Foray nodded at the sky.

A full moon was rising to light the long spreads and the low hills, the waiting sand traps and the small lake. A wind rustled in the oak trees.

"I'll be damned," whispered Gingrich.

He let himself be led out the wire screen door to the first tee.

"You first," said Foray, and placed the ball and tee for him.

Gingrich watched, almost frozen.

When Foray stood back, Gingrich took steady aim, raised his club, and brought it down like a blow of summer lightning. Bam!

He watched the ball fly like a lovely white bird up toward the moon and down toward the fairway green.

"Son of a bitch!" he cried.

"Oh, oh," he cried again. "Son of a bitch!"

"Fore!" Foray shouted, though there was no one out there on the course to harm. Or maybe there was someone way out there, a shadow.

"Fore!" he said.

My Son,
Max

I HAVE THIS wonderful ability to read lips. It came from growing up with two boy cousins who had hearing problems, and they passed the "language" on to me at an early age. What the hell, I thought, aged nine, if you're going to be around boys like this, you might as well steal secrets. For I had found that, across parlors, or in halls, I could tune in on people and they were never the wiser. So I have led a secret life and never told anyone that the merest syllable dropped from a lip forty or eighty yards away was mine. No silent word moves through the world without entering my eye to make me smile.

So, armed with this ability, I often dine alone; for, in truth, I am dining with families. Any mouth that I choose to watch becomes my brother, sister, father, mother, or old maid aunt. And if I choose not to "listen" I merely scan my wine, my

steak, and my eating utensils, or find fascination in chandeliers.

This one night, I did not need, nor did I want, chandeliers.

I had just finished ordering when a family of three arrived
and sat directly opposite me, in such a way that if I missed any
of the sweets or poisons dropping from their mouths, in pan-
tomime, the rest I might catch in either ear.

They were a handsome father and mother in their forties,
and a son of some twenty years, equally handsome, or, no,
beautiful. So beautiful that you knew without knowing that
every time he came down to earth there was an eager but
soon dissatisfied woman reaching up to grab or an even more
ravenous man seizing and keeping.

So it was very sad for me to glance up from time to time
to see this man and wife and their lighter-than-air child
examining their menus as if a list of their lives was there; the
mother calm, the father looking as if he had been hit by life
and sunk. In every glance at his son was not recrimination,
but a terrible sad acceptance. The son was obviously the only
son, and there would be no marriage, no children, no passing
on of the name. Everything ended here tonight, at this table,
with this child, much loved, but unaccommodating to life.
The father looked to be one of those who had rarely stormed
at fate, cursed, or dared to throw the son out. His was a deep
misery from which he might never surface. He had so looked
forward to a lineage, some sort of family, no matter how spare.

Wine was ordered, poured, and as the silent three drank,
their faces came to a focus.

Oh, good Lord, yes, I said to myself. They dined here

about a year ago! And this, by God, is the second chapter. I'll find out what's happened since. It's the despair family, only this time, they do not look quite as despairing!

I settled in, watching their mouths, occasionally catching a drift of words, and was soon re-immersed in their incredible lives. Soon, I was remembering it all.

A year ago had been a disastrous, half-eaten meal, from which the father had risen, with a distempered and multicolored face, only to have the mother run out after him begging him to return, while the son slowly finished a glass of wine, eyes down, and after a long while, very much alone, paid the bill and, it almost seemed, sneaked away.

Now, watching the family—their name was Robinson, I heard the headwaiter say—it seemed to me that they all looked younger than last January. That night long ago, I had watched them age with shock, horror, incredulity, and then an anger that leaned into madness. At least on the father's part. His face had got redder and redder, while his wife's had got paler and paler, and the son's complexion took on some of each, mottled and blotched with confusion.

The son had realized, too late, that confession was not good for the soul. He had described his hidden life honestly and completely and seen his parents suffering instant devastation.

Now, as I waited, I counted the glasses of wine the father took to solidify his will and loosen his tongue. He was almost beaming when he leaned forward, his enunciation so pronounced it was easy for me to read his lips.

"Now listen to me," he said. "I have something to tell you." He poured more wine for the two of them. "You recall, our dinner here, oh, last New Year's, and here it is nearly Christmas, yes? Well. Back then, Ronald, you admitted to the sort of life you've been leading. To say that we were stunned would be putting it mildly. Not that we hadn't suspected, but you always chide yourself back into ignorance. After all, you think, it can't happen in *our* family. And then when we met several of your friends, the safe fell off the building and we were crushed. Sorry to admit, it's true. Anyway, it took me a month to get back up on my feet, lying awake nights thinking wild thoughts, and then one afternoon in late March having another safe dropped on me. Only this time, it was a wonderfully incredible blow. An inspiration. I had been running around in the rat maze for weeks, with no way out. After all, you are our only son. No use convincing you that you should get married, put up a front, have children. I don't know what the percentages are in marriages like that. I'm sure they occur and we never know it, or find out about it, later, when there's a separation or a divorce. Anyway, I knew after several false starts there was no use bargaining a future with you when you were not listening."

The young man put down his empty wineglass.

"Lord, Dad," he said, "get on with it."

"Am I taking too long?" asked the father, sitting back, surprised at himself.

His wife said, "Yes, dear, a bit. Where is all this leading?"

The father ducked his head in sudden embarrassment, then looked up, saw the empty wineglasses, and refilled them.

"Well, it's this. Do you know that Miss Gilham in my office?"

"The pretty one, the one with the legs," said his wife.

"You have noticed, then." He ducked his head again, and color crept into his face.

"Good Lord, I think I know what's coming," said the young man.

"No you don't. Not by half!"

"I think I do," said his wife.

"No, nor you, either. You see, it's very complicated, yet at the same time simple. I gave her a year off!"

"To do what?" asked his wife, puzzled.

"At full salary. To have a baby. Mine."

"Hold on!" cried the wife.

But he was on his feet.

"Be right back." And he was gone toward the men's room, leaving his wife and son with a large black safe neatly dropped and crashed in their midst now.

"Jesus," said the young man at last. "He's crazy."

"I wish he were," said the mother.

They sat and waited until the father returned, sat down, without looking at them, drank more wine, and said, "Well?"

"What do you mean, well?" said the son. "You toss a bomb in our faces and run. Is this some crummy joke? To say all this in front of one of us would be bad enough. But in front of both of us? Christ."

"It was the only way," the father admitted. "Facing you one at a time would have been an ordeal. This way, somehow, it's cushioned. Now, before either of you says anything more—"

"We haven't said anything yet," said the wife.

"I am not leaving home," said the husband. "I do not want a divorce, I still love you very much, and I have not seen my secretary again, except to give her her weekly check."

"I don't believe it," said the wife.

"I will not touch the woman again, ever. The child is due to be born at Christmas—splendid timing. And, most important, grandest of all, it is going to be a boy!"

He sat back smiling around at his audience, waiting for their response.

The wife sighed and shadows passed over her face, without leaving a trace of something to say.

The son pushed back from the table and tossed his napkin on his plate.

"Is this supposed to be some sort of insult to me?" he asked.

"No. Only a response," said the father. "I couldn't sit still with no future. I was so damned unhappy I had to react. And then suddenly it hit me: start a new life, find the right woman, have a boy child, give it my name, and, twenty years from now—bam. Immortality. More families, more children. God's in his heaven, all's right with the world!"

"And this stupid woman has gone along with your dumb idea!" cried the son.

"She is not stupid and she has gone along. She is *muy simpatica*, as they say. She saw my deeps of depression, locked in the graveyard as it were, with a living son who was, in effect, dead. She knew how to cry, 'Lazarus, come forth!' And I left the graveyard. And twenty years from now, I will be, well, let me see, nearly seventy, that's not bad, seventy, and happy. I will give the boy our family name, of course. You need never see him, don't be afraid of that. Now, the next and final thing is, do we go on as before? Does my wife still love me in spite of this madness? Will my son speak to me, or take affront and move out? I hope both answers from the two of you will be made out of some lopsided understanding and much love. Ah, here comes the dessert cart, not a moment too soon."

While the father indicated and accepted a strawberry tart the son leaned forward.

"Do you have a name for this—this—" He stopped and flushed.

"Bastard?"

"No!"

"You were going to say 'bastard.' Say it."

"Bastard."

"There, feel better? Yes, I have a name! Maximilian—"

"Maximilian!?"

"Max. My son Max. God, that sounds good, don't you agree? A name like that? Royalty. It has a regal sound. Max, my son."

"And will he move into my room when I move out?"

"Are you moving out? No need. I wouldn't dream of burdening your mama. Besides, my secretary is pleased to be a mother and looks forward to eighteen or twenty years of work and play with the child. I will visit him, of course, and take him out six or seven times a week, so he has a proper father."

There was a still longer silence as coffee was placed on the table.

"Well, Mother," said Ronald, "aren't you going to say something?"

"Yes." The mother frowned and then said, "I'll be God-damned."

This time it was the son who plunged out of the restaurant. He sailed out, a trim ship in a high wind, his beautiful nose prowing the air. His mother ran after.

The father stayed, maundering over the bill, then, with some leisure, finished the last of the wine, rose, and walked past me. He stopped with his back to me. At first I didn't think he was speaking to me, but then he repeated his question: "You read lips, don't you?"

"What?"

I turned and he looked at me with steady gray eyes.

"Raised in a family of deaf-mutes?"

"Sort of," I admitted uneasily.

"It's all right. You a writer?"

"How did you guess?"

"Anyone that watches lips that closely has got to be something. It was quite a story, wasn't it?"

"I didn't catch it all," I lied.

The father laughed quietly and nodded. "Yes, you did. But it's okay. None of it's true."

I almost dropped my dessert spoon. "What!?"

"I had to think of something. I suppose it's been collecting up all year. All of a sudden, tonight, bam! You going to write it down when you get home?"

"No. Yes. I don't know. But—"

"But what?"

I swallowed with difficulty. "I—I just wish it were true."

The father pulled a cigar out of his pocket, looked at it, found a lighter, lit it, smoked a big puff out on the air, and looked at the elusive stuff shaping and reshaping itself and blowing away into nothing. His eyes were watchful and growing wet, with all this.

"So do I, son," he said, and walked away. "So do I."

After a long moment I ordered another bottle of wine. When it was opened and poured, the waiter said, "Think you can finish that much?"

"I'm going to try," I said. "Let me try."

The
F. Scott / Tolstoy / Ahab
Accumulator

"WHY WOULD YOU want to rewire, revise, and reconceive your Time Machine?" said my friend Billy Barlow.

"It's one thing," I replied, "to run back in time and place new printings of books by Melville, Poe, and Wilde on their deathbeds and wake them to see their glory. But . . ."

I paused.

"But another thing," I finished, "to seek unhappy people and make them happy. Think of all the lost writers who wrote beautifully and lived miserably."

"All writers are lost," said Billy. "And miserable."

"I'll change that," I said.

"Bull," Billy said. "How, oh Lord God of miracles? With three wishes on a genie lamp? With—"

"Shut up. See that huge device stranded in the library?"

"That giant moth? Does it flap its wings?"

"It hums under its breath and vanishes."

"The louder it hums the farther back in Time you go?"

"Right. Here's my list of lost souls."

Billy scowled at the list. "Hemingway? Melville? No way. Tolstoy? Why? F. Scott Fitzgerald and Zelda? Drunks!"

"Gimme that!" I grabbed the list, sat in the machine, cursed, pulled a lever, and said: "I'm not here."

The machine hummed.

And I wasn't.

THE MACHINE SETTLED as gently as a great cellophane butterfly by Papa's house in Idaho. God, I thought, what do I say?

I pried myself from the trembling wings, and had walked up on the porch to knock when the door opened. Hemingway stood there.

He looked sleepless. His broad pale face somehow expected me and here I was. He turned and walked back to a hall table, sat down, and nodded to a chair. I advanced, staring at what lay gleaming on the table: a steel African hunting rifle, the sort that knocked echoes off Kilimanjaro, and once killed elephants as white as the hot Kenya dust. Nearby lay a double-barreled shotgun.

I sat and saw on the table two glasses of clear grappa. I took one glass while Papa slugged his back.

"Well?" he said.

I ignored the table and said: "Don't."

"Don't what?"

"Whatever you were going to do."

"I wasn't going to do anything," said Papa.

"You were thinking it."

"You read minds?"

"No. Just some of your stories. There was a doctor in one of them, your father? We all know what happened to him."

"We all know that," said Papa.

"Some say you still have his weapon."

"Somewhere."

"Well, let's not mince words. If you do something silly, people will guess all the wrong motives."

"There are no wrong motives for getting out when the getting's good."

"No. It's not what you think, it's what the academics write. They'll pee on your grave, then change your title to *The Sun Never Rises.*"

"It can't be touched. What I was once, for a while. I hate to brag, but . . ."

"Why not? You are Papa."

Papa almost smiled, then lit a cigarette.

"How long have you read me?"

"Since algebra, behind the book. Eighth grade."

"Great place, behind other books. In *The Sun Also Rises,* what was that to you?"

"Big doors opening, big gates, a whole world pouring out with places, pretty women, and toreros, both with nice backsides, and how to survive not being a man anymore."

"That's a lot to know when you're a kid."

"I was hungry. Don't change the subject. If you leave now . . ."

"I haven't left yet."

"They'll eat your entrails, Papa."

"If they tear them out."

"Eat your guts, throw them up, and eat them again."

"Will they leave my manhood?"

"That goes first, so you can't fight."

"Hyenas, eh?"

"Dingos, buzzards, *zopilotes,* sharks."

"The whole Harvard English Department?"

"And Ohio State."

"That's some list." Papa stared into my face. "And who are you to make it? Why are you here? A nut?"

"A lover."

"Blush when you say that."

"Why should I, when it's true?"

"Hell. A true believer."

"No, someone who loves writing. Not fine. Just good."

"Always was," said Papa quietly.

"And you can be good again."

"With a ruptured spleen, two broken ribs, a fractured fibula, and a cracked skull?"

"All that. Let the medics really cure your ribs, your leg, your head. With your body fixed, your nerves renewed, and the pain gone . . ."

"My writing will come back, too?"

"It must."

"I don't know if I can wait," he said. "It's bad to get up early, stand at your typewriter and work, then find it's nothing and take a bottle to bed. Who do I do this for?"

"For yourself. Hell, no. Me."

"Selfish bastard."

"Damn right."

He stared at me.

"Jesus, go write a book on philosophy."

"No, just hygiene, if you'll listen."

Papa glanced at the door.

"Get outta here," he said.

"If I can take the guns."

"You crazy?"

"No, you. Pain makes you crazy. Your writing didn't fail. It stopped because you were sick. You can't think when pain cuts in. Ever try to write hungover? Never works. The critics knock your writing and forget that plane crash in Africa that wrecked it, left you mad. But maybe next week you'll wake with no knife in your chest, no bad leg, no headache, and know how mad you were."

"Am I mad now?"

"With yourself, and me for telling you."

"You finished?"

"No, empty, Papa. Just remember, if you're gone next year they'll call your story 'The Short Unhappy Life of Francis Macomber.' Then *For Whom No Bell Tolls*. See?"

"I don't need a third crash."

"Well, then." I reached for the guns.

"Don't," said Papa. "I'd find another way."

"Take four aspirin. Kill the pain. I'll call tomorrow."

I walked to the front door.

"What's your name?" he called.

I told him.

"Have a good life," he said.

"No, Papa. You."

I went out the door.

I was about fifty feet from the house when I thought I heard a loud sound, shut my eyes, and ran.

THE VAST MONARCH wings whispered, folded, stopped.

I looked in through a twilight door and saw:

An old man stamping, stamping, stamping forms in the customs shed at Nantucket.

I drew close and said, "Mr. Melville?"

He lifted the blind gaze of an ancient sea tortoise.

"Sir?" he said.

I suddenly did not fit my skin within my clothes.

"Sir, are you hungry?"

The old man searched his appetite.

I said, "May we dine and perhaps stroll the wharves?" I raised a small sack of apples and oranges, plus, in the other hand, a nameless book. He studied that book and at last took an immense time shrugging on an overcoat and let himself be led out into the clouded light of a sunless day. Facing away from the sea, he said: "You are a critic? From Boston?"

"No," I said, "a mere reader."

"There are no mere readers," said the old man. "You are either out of a library or safely in. Book dust fills that air.

Inhaled, it firms a man's bones, brightens his eye, tunes his ear. Thus a man is renewed breath by breath, when he swims the library deeps where multitudinous blind creatures wait. Your mind says rise and they swarm, overbrim, drown you with their stuffs. Drowned but alive, you are the atoll it floods without end. Thus, you are no mere reader, but a survivor of tides that surf from Shakespeare to Pope to Molière. Those lighthouses of being. Go there to survive the storms.

"That is," he caught himself, "if I shut up and you had time to read." He let his faint smile fade. "Why are we here on this dock?"

"Sir," I said. "There is the sea, where you should go forever."

"Swim round the Cape? Surprise China?"

"Why not?"

"Do you see this old man's hand palsied from stamping and stamping the damned inspection forms?"

"No," I said, "I see a sailor at sea with a dark islander, all tattoos, and a lost first mate whose captain struck God's sun when it insulted him." I continued: "Oh, dear Melville, stay off the land. The sea is yours. You're like that ancient god who, thrown down, revived his life. Held high, he lost his power. On earth, his life grew tall. But your power is water! Cast off now, be a sea beast reborn to compass points, arms spread to smite hurricanes from white whales' flukes. Take St. Elmo's fires to shave. Earth, shore, town, and docks are tombs, coffin law-sheds, sunless days, lost burials. Earthbound, you dig your grave. Curse the land, throw down the customs stamp, be young ape-clambering the mast to dive, swim fast, the fair isles wait. I'm shut."

"Shakespeare opened you."

"Forgive."

"Forgive me, then, who gave the White Whale's oil to light the towns. Be you a Christian?"

"God counts me in."

"Then Christian soul, be still as I judge ships and guess the tides."

Old Melville stared long at the horizon, then gazed at the salt-worn fronts of the customhouse which knew no sound but the eternal stamping and stamping of sea forms out and in.

"Jack!" I whispered. Melville flinched. I caught my breath and thought: Jack, young Christ, far from Galilee, fine of form and face, Jack, good shipmate, like the morning sun. And Hawthorne? Do we kidnap and jog along him with? Such talks you'd have! I'll serve him for our feast of Time, while Jack thrusts his gaze to seize your heart and crack your eyes. Hawthorne for loud noons. Jack for speechless midnights, endless dawns.

"Jack," whispered Herman Melville. "Alive?"

"I can make him live."

"Your God machine, does it bless or curse? Does it create or act Time's infidel?"

"It's nameless, sir. A centrifuge to spin off years to make us young."

"Can you do this?"

"And win King Richard's crown? Yes!"

"Ah, God." Melville's voice broke as he pulled at his feet. "I cannot move!"

"Try!"

"It's late," he said. "I'm neither fish nor fowl. On land, Stonehenge. At sea I sink. Is there no place between?"

"Here." I touched my head. "And here," I touched my heart.

The old man's eyes burned with tears.

"Oh! If I could live in that head or hide in that breast!"

"You are safely there."

"I accept a night's lodging," he wept.

"No, *Pequod*'s captain," I said. "A thousand days."

"This joy breaks me! Hold!"

I held his quaking elbows.

"You," he said, "have opened the library and let me breathe my past. Am I taller? Straighter? Is my voice clear?"

"Most clear."

"My hands?"

"Are the hands of a sailor newborn."

"Stay off land?"

"Stay off."

"But look." He pointed. "My legs are anchors! Much thanks for your miracle of words. Oh, thanks . . ."

And he wandered off into the customs shed.

I looked in upon this old man a thousand miles distant on the dark earth, saw his hand fly up, down, up, down, stamping the forms, eyes shut, gone blind, as I backed off to feel the huge wings brush my neck. I spun to let the great moth take me.

"O, Herman, stay!" I cried, but the shed was gone.

And I was spun forth in another time, a house, a door opened and shut, a small round man confronting me.

"How," he said, "did you get in?"

"Down the chimney, under the door. And you are?"

"Count Leo Tolstoy!"

"Of *War and Peace?*"

"Is there another!?" he exclaimed. "How did you enter? For what purpose?"

"To help you run away!"

"Run—?"

"Away," I said, "from home. For you are crazed. Your wife is berserk with jealousy."

Count Leo Tolstoy froze. "How—?"

"It's all in the books."

"There are no books!"

"Not now, but soon! To claim your wife accused the chambermaids, the kitchen help, the gardener's daughters, your accountant's mistress, the milkman's wife, your niece!"

"Stop!" cried Count Leo Tolstoy. "I refuse those beds!"

"They lie?"

"Yes, maybe, no, how dare you!"

"Because your wife threatens to tear the sheets, burn the bed, lock the door, decapitate your modus operandi."

"No, yes! Guilty, innocent, guilty, innocent! Damn! Guilty! What a wife. Repeat!"

"Home. Run away from it."

"That is what boys do!"

"Yes!"

"And you'd have me act half a life younger? You are a lunatic of solutions."

"Better than a maniac of punishments."

"Lower your voice!" he whispered. "She's in the next room."

"Then, let's go!"

"She has stolen my underwear!"

"Wash and wear on the way."

"To?"

"Anywhere!"

"But how long do I hide?"

"Until she swoons, apoplectic!"

"Superb! Who are you?"

"The only man on earth who has read *War and Peace* and remembered the names. Shall I list them?"

At this a fierce blow hit a far door.

"Thank God," I said, "it's locked."

"What shall I pack?"

"A toothbrush! Quick!"

I threw the outer door wide. Count Leo Tolstoy stared out.

"What is that mist made of transparent leaves and milkweed?"

"Salvation!"

"It is beautiful."

There was more banging on the door, a bray like an elephant.

"The maniac," he cried.

"Do you wear running shoes?"

"I . . ."

"Run!"

He ran. The machine enfolded him.

The library door burst wide. A face of fury raged, an open furnace. "Where is he?" she cried.

"Who?" I said and vanished.

PERHAPS I MATERIALIZED to Billy Barlow, perhaps he materialized to me. But suddenly my machine took root in my library as Billy was glancing up Tolstoy, Melville, and Papa.

"Two losses and a win!" I said.

Billy shut Melville, closed Papa, smiled at Tolstoy.

"I made him leave madame," I said.

"Did she enact *Anna Karenina?*"

"Throw herself under a train? No."

"Pity. You off on more travels? White House, April '65, maybe. Steal Mary Todd Lincoln's theater tickets?"

"And risk her bite? No. Gangway!"

THE GOLDEN WINGS soughed to touch by the waters of the marble fount near the Hotel Plaza. The fountains lifted quiet jets on a summer night. In the fount, wading, stagger- ing, laughing, martini glasses raised to the moon, swayed a handsome man in a drenched tuxedo and a lovely woman in a silver gown. They whooped and hollered until my shout.

"Time!" I cried. "Zelda! Scottie! Everyone out!"

Well, What Do You Have to Say for Yourself?

"WELL, WHAT DO you have to say for yourself?"

He looked at the telephone he had just picked up, and put it back near his ear.

"What time is it?" he asked.

"Aren't you wearing your watch?"

"It's by my bed."

"It's six thirty-five."

"My God, so early, and the first thing you say is, 'What do you have to say for yourself?' I'm not awake yet."

"Go make some coffee and talk. What's the hotel like?"

"At six thirty-five in the morning, what's the hotel like? I don't like hotels. Three bad nights now with no sleep."

"How do you think I've been sleeping?"

"Look," he said, "I just got out of bed, let me put on my glasses and look at my watch, can I come over?"

"What for, what's the use?"

"You asked what I had to say, I want to say it."

"Then say it."

"Not on the phone. It'll take some time. Give me half an hour. Fifteen minutes. All right, then, ten."

"Five," she said, "and talk fast."

She hung up.

At ten minutes after eight he watched her pour coffee and let him pick up his own cup. She crossed her arms over her breasts and waited, looking at the ceiling.

"It's already five minutes and all we've done is pour the coffee," he said.

She looked at her watch, silently.

"Okay, okay," he said, and burnt his lips taking the coffee, putting it down, rubbing his mouth, shutting his eyes, clenching his hands together in a kind of tight prayer mode.

"Well?" she said.

"Don't say it again," he said, eyes shut. "Here goes. All men. All men are alike."

"You can say that again," she said.

He waited, eyes shut, to be sure she was done speaking.

"At least we agree on one thing," he said. "All men are alike. I'm like every other man that ever lived. They are all like me. That has never changed, that will never change. That is a given. That is a rock bottom basic genetic truth."

"How did genetics get into this?"

He had to force himself to remain silent, and then he said, "When God touched Adam, the genetics were put there. Can I continue?"

Her silence was a kind of grim affirmative.

"Let's agree for the moment, we can argue it later, that all the billions of men that ever grew up racing and yelling and behaving like lunatics were one and the same, some smaller, some taller, none different. I'm one of those."

He waited again, but since there was no comment he clenched his eyes, worked his fingers, interlaced, and went on.

"Along with all those circus animals, the other humans came, the ones nearer that name human, who had to put up with the carnival atmosphere, clean the cages, pick up the cave or the parlor, raise the kids, go mad, recover, go mad again, make do."

"It's getting late."

"It's only eight-fifteen in the morning. Give me until eight-thirty, for God's sake. Please."

She was silent again, so he went on.

"So you have a few hundred thousand years of getting out of caves and hunting for food and settling down. That's all pretty recent. I'm writing an essay now called 'Too Soon from the Cave, Too Far Away from the Stars.'" Silence. "But that's neither here nor there, sorry. But after tens of thousands of years of kindergarten turmoil, the women, gone bald from being trekked across country by their long hair, bruised and beaten, finally said, 'Enough! Stand still, sit straight, pull up your socks, now hear this!'

"The men, for that's what they finally became, not cave dwellers, not absolutely dumb yahoos, sat straight, pulled up their dirty socks, and listened. And do you know what they heard?"

A silence that suggested her arms were still crossed firmly over her breasts.

"What they heard was amazing. It was the marriage ceremony. Yes, that was it. Primitive at first, but it got larger and clearer and better. And the men, struck dumb, actually listened. At first out of curiosity, and then, though they wouldn't admit it, impressed. It had a kind of ring to it. It got through to those uncaged beasts and some of them nodded and then, after a while, all of them nodded intently and indicated, hell, why not give it a try.

"There had to be some way to calm us down, make us behave, for a little while, sometimes for good," he said. "And we all stood there, a few to start, more to follow by the dozens and thousands and finally millions, young men full of pomegranate seeds by the billion, answering questions, nodding, saying yes, but in their hearts wondering how in hell they were going to live up to all this, these fine words, their grand sentiments, and their brides beside them crying and the brides' fathers behind them like the Great Wall of China, doubtful but in hopes.

"And I remember standing there by you and thinking this is ridiculous, it won't work, it can't last, I love her, sure, I really love her, but somewhere up the line, who can say how or where or why, I'll fall off the wagon, like everyone else, and make a damn fool, clumsy ass, of myself, and hope she won't know or if she does, ignore, or if not ignore, somewhere in between. And a mess of worms inside me, I gave all the right answers but kept my own questions, next thing I knew we stepped out in a summer rain of rice.

"Well," he said, and looked at his hands that had been interlaced, but now the fingers hung free and his hands were there, palms up, as if to receive something, they knew not what. "That's it, except to say in the next five hundred years or a thousand or a million, no matter where we go, I guess it's back to the Moon and then out to make camps on Mars and maybe someday some planet near Alpha Centauri, but no matter how far we go or how great our aims and announcements, we will never change. Men will go on being men, stupid, arrogant, strong-willed, stubborn, reckless, destructive, murderous, but sometimes librarians and poets, kite fliers and boys who see things in clouds, nephew to Robert Frost and Shakespeare, but still not always dependable, soft-hearted under the skin maybe, capable of tears if the children should die and life be over, always looking at the next field where the grass is greener and the milk is free, fixed on a Moon crater or stationed on one of Saturn's moons, but the same beast that yelled out of the cave half a million years ago, not much different, and the other half of the human race there staring at him and asking him to listen to the wedding rites with half a heart and half an ear, and sometimes, sometimes he listens."

He paused, fearful of her silence, but went on: "I often wonder, don't you, at all the houses I pass on the way to work, down the hill in the morning, and I think, whoever's there, I hope they're happy, I hope it isn't an empty house or a silent house, and coming home at night, passing the same houses I think, are they still happy, are they silent, is there any kind of stir or yell? And then I see a basketball hoop in front of one house and I think there's a son there, there's a change, maybe.

And another house, there's rice thrown in the drive, and there's a daughter, happy maybe, no way to know. But every morning I think the very same thing. I hope they're happy, oh God, please, I hope it's so."

He stopped, breathless, and waited, eyes shut.

"And that's the way you see yourself?" she said.

"Approximately," he said.

"And all those other men everywhere."

"In all time, yes, by the million."

"You claim protection from them?"

"No, we're out in the open where you can get at us."

"No protective coloration?"

"None of that."

"All the same?"

"None different."

"You're not giving us women much choice."

"There's very little. You take us as you find us. Or you don't take us at all. With you, it's different. We look at you and see girlfriends, lovers, wives, mothers, teachers, nurses. You have so many sides. We have one if we're lucky, the work that we do, not much else."

He waited.

"Are you done?" she said.

"I think so. Yes. I think that's it."

Silence, and then, "Is this some sort of excuse?"

"No."

"Are you rationalizing?"

"I don't think so."

"An alibi then, for all of you?"

"No alibi, no."

"Are you asking to be understood?"

"I'm not quite sure. Something like that."

"Are you asking for sympathy?"

"Never."

"Compassion?"

"Oh, God no."

"Empathy?"

"All those words are too strong."

"What then, what?"

"I just wanted you to listen is all."

"I've done that."

"And thanks."

He opened his eyes and saw that where she sat her eyes were closed now, but her arms, her blessed arms, had fallen free and down off her breasts.

Silently, he arose and moved toward the door and opened it and went out.

He had just closed the front door to his hotel apartment when the phone rang. He stood over it, weaving, until it had rung four or five times. Then, carefully, he picked it up.

"You're a rat," she said, a long way off.

"I know," he said.

"You're a bastard," she said.

"That, too," he said.

"And a no-good bounder and a cad."

"All those."

"And a son of a bitch."

"That almost goes without saying."

"But," she said.

He waited. He heard her take in a long breath.

"But," she said, and there was a long pause, "I love you."

"Thank God," he whispered.

"Come home," she said.

"I will," he said.

"And don't start blubbering," she said. "I can't stand men who cry."

"I won't," he said.

"And when you come in," she said.

"Yes?"

"Don't forget to lock the door."

"It's as good as locked," he said.

Diane de Forêt

I T   W A S   A T twilight in the autumn of 1989, in the hour of
the closing of the graveyard in Paris, when I, overlooked by the
guards who were ushering out the last visitors, came upon the
low marble tomb of Diane de Forêt, she of the forest, and
stood listening to the last calls of the guards and the shutting
of the gates. The thought that I might be trapped in Père
Lachaise for the night did not bother me, for I saw laid out
before me the most beautiful tomb, the most radiant marble
carving, I had ever witnessed in any graveyard in all my life.

The tomb itself was a marble lid some six feet long and
perhaps eighteen inches high, and upon the lid, in gossamer
folds of marble, her delicate hands laid across her frail bosom,
was the figure of a timeless mythic beauty. Hers was the face
of a young woman, no more than eighteen, with a fair brow,
fine cheekbones, and a mouth that seemed shaped almost to
smile, disregarding time, this place, and the weather.

I stood for a long while, stricken with those pangs which, in the life of the flesh, can only be recognized as the start of something as mysterious as hate, fear, or joy, while its name is love.

All those elements that move their chemistries in us partake of the same mystery and break off to become special emotions, neither summed nor solved, only to be accepted, enjoyed or spurned swiftly, seeking other chemistries, other emotions.

Now, as I shadowed the tomb with the last of the sun's light, I swayed and almost fell at my terrible surprise; this youngness, this beauty from my past.

The vertigo subsided. I read these words above her pale brow:

DIANE DE FORÊT
Born 1800. Died 1818.

Oh, God, I whispered. Lost before I was born.
More words were carved in marble below:

So quickly she ran that only Death could catch her.
My fortune was to know her for an hour and love her,
in my life, forever.

Following were the initials *R.C.* and a postscript:

Who has carved this relief to shape her memory.

Ah, Lord, I heard myself say, there are two lovers here, not only the child bride but her beloved, the sculptor who day by day raised this bosom, these hands, this sleeping face up from the stone. How many years had passed and how often had he come to drop his tears upon this silence?

Not knowing, I leaned close to memorize each fine detail of fair brow, delicate nostril, and half-smiling lips, rained on by storms but undissolved by time.

In doing so, my tears, blinding me, fell upon the marble face.

As if at a trick of vision, her features seemed to melt instantly, then freeze before I could pull back, breathless.

My tears had touched her lids. It seemed she wept. The tears were now not mine but hers, and moved down her cheeks, to touch her lips, which, touched, caused me to doubt my senses. For the faintest murmur, the merest whisper, drifted up from the pale marble face.

"Yes?" the whisper said.

Silence. I waited, frozen in place.

The lips shadowed themselves: "Who's there?"

No, no, I thought. Not so!

"Well?" came the whisper. A tear trembled on her cold mouth.

At last I said, "It's only me."

"If that is true," came the whisper, "where have you been?"

"I—"

"I've been waiting for you," came the whisper.

"I—" Again, I could not go on.

"It's been so long," said the voice hid in the face, within the stone. "Why have you abandoned me?"

You don't understand, I thought, we are separated by death. Yours. And then, his, your lover's, a long time ago.

At last I murmured: "What can I say?"

"Something. Anything." A shadow crossed her mouth.

"I am here now."

"Thank God."

"Do you forgive me?"

A leaf fell and touched her cheek, quickly. "Oh, yes. Now that you're here, all the past years are nothing. Say more. Anything. Something."

I took a breath and said, "I love you."

"Oh, yes!" came the cry. I feared that the tomb might burst and a woman-child erupt from this cold chrysalis. "Now I know what I was waiting for! Again!"

"I love you," I said, and it was the truth.

"Oh, yes!" came the ardent voice again. "And this time is it really true? By the way you say it; true? Dear God, take my soul! With those words, let me die!"

"But—" I exclaimed, and stopped.

You are already dead, I thought.

"Oh," the voice went on in breathless haste beneath her name and face, "is there anything more beautiful than love? To love is to live forever, or die and recall love for eternity. We never tire of hearing it. There is no burden. One rises up with each time it is said. So, please . . ."

"I love you," I said.

And from within the tomb, a trembling pulse, a knock of life against the downpressed lid.

"Yet," her quiet voice said, "we must speak of other things. Since last we met and talked, what?"

One hundred and seventy-one years? I thought.

"It is a long while," I said. "Forgive me."

"But, why did you run away? After that, I didn't want to live. Did you go round the world and see places and forget?"

And returned, I thought, to find you here, and built your tomb.

"And what will you be doing now?" her voice said.

"I am a writer," I said. "I will be writing a story about a graveyard and a beautiful woman and a lost lover returned."

"Surely not a graveyard? Why not somewhere else?"

"I'll try."

"Love," said her voice, "why so sad? Let me comfort you."

I sat on the edge of the tomb.

"There," she whispered. "Take my hand."

I placed my hand atop her folded hands.

"Oh, your hands are so cold. How can I warm them?"

"Say as I said to you."

" 'I love you'?"

"Yes."

"I love you!"

A moment and then, "That's better. Warmness. And yet there is something you haven't told me. Say it now."

"A long time ago," I said, "you were eighteen. Now, more than a century later, you are still eighteen."

"How can that be? Eighteen?"

"There is no age, no time, where you are. You will always be young."

"Where am I then that keeps me young?"

I could hardly breathe, but managed to go on: "Touch above you, below, and around. Then you will know what keeps you."

In the following silence, the very last of the sun faded from Père Lachaise. More leaves fell.

The faint heartbeat beneath the lid grew ever fainter, as did her voice.

"Oh, no," she mourned. "And is it true?"

"It is."

"But you have come to save me!"

"No, dear Diane de Forêt, only to visit."

"But you said you loved me!"

"And I do. Oh, yes, God yes, I do."

"Well, then?"

"You still don't understand. I am not who you think I am. But you are someone I hoped to meet one day."

"Impossible!"

"Yes, which is why it is so wonderful."

"You were waiting all these years, just as I was waiting?"

"So it seems."

"Are you glad you waited?"

"Now, yes. But it was lonely."

"And from now on, what?"

"You still don't understand," I said. "My age."

"What has that to do with us?"

"I am," I said at last, "seventy-three years old."

"That much?"

"That," I said.

"But your voice is young."

"Because I am talking to you."

There was a sound beneath my hand upon her hands. Was she weeping? I waited and listened.

"Dear one," she said at last, "how strange. We are on opposite ends of a balancing-board. I rise, you fall, you rise, I fall. Will we ever truly meet?"

"Only here," I said.

Her voice quickened. "Then you will come back? You won't lie to me again and leave?"

"I promise."

"Come close," she whispered. "I cannot speak. Help me."

I bent near to let my tears fall again on her face. Her voice, refreshed, said, "While you still have tears to help me speak, it's time."

"To say goodbye?"

"Seventy and three years? Do you have someone beyond the gate to go to?"

"Sadly, no."

"Then, you will return. And bring your tears?"

"They will not stop."

"Come again. There is much to tell."

"About Death?"

"Ah, no. Eternity. All. All of it. Eternity, dear friend. Eternity. I will teach you. Your tears have stopped. So must I. Goodbye."

I rose.

"Farewell, Diane de Forêt," I said.

A leaf fell shadowing her face. Farewell.

I ran to shake the gates and call the guards, half wishing to be free, half hoping to stay here forever.

Just in time, the guards arrived. They unlocked the gate.

The Cricket
on the Hearth

THE DOOR SLAMMED and John Martin was out of his hat and coat and past his wife as fluently as a magician en route to a better illusion. He produced the newspaper with a dry whack as he slipped his coat into the closet like an abandoned ghost and sailed through the house, scanning the news, his nose guessing at the identity of supper, talking over his shoulder, his wife following. There was still a faint scent of the train and the winter night about him. In his chair he sensed an unaccustomed silence resembling that of a birdhouse when a vulture's shadow looms; all the robins, sparrows, mockingbirds quiet. His wife stood whitely in the door, not moving.

"Come sit down," said John Martin. "What're you doing? God, don't stare as if I were dead. What's new? Not that there's ever anything new, of course. What do you think of those fathead city councilmen today? More taxes, more every goddamn thing."

"John!" cried his wife. "Don't!"

"Don't what?"

"Don't talk that way. It isn't safe!"

"For God's sake, not safe? Is this Russia or is this our own house?!"

"Not exactly."

"Not exactly?"

"There's a bug in our house," she whispered.

"A bug?" He leaned forward, exasperated.

"You know. Detective talk. When they hide a microphone somewhere you don't know, they call it a bug, I think," she whispered even more quietly.

"Have you gone nuts?"

"I thought I might have when Mrs. Thomas told me. They came last night while we were out and asked Mrs. Thomas to let them use her garage. They set up their equipment there and strung wires over here, the house is wired, the bug is in one or maybe all of the rooms."

She was standing over him now and bent to whisper in his ear.

He fell back. "Oh, no!"

"Yes!"

"But we haven't done anything—"

"Keep your voice down!" she whispered.

"Wait!" he whispered back, angrily, his face white, red, then white again. "Come on!"

Out on the terrace, he glanced around and swore. "Now say the whole damn thing again! They're using the neighbor's garage to hide their equipment? The FBI?"

"Yes, yes, oh it's been awful! I didn't want to call, I was afraid your wire was tapped, too."

"We'll see, dammit! Now!"

"Where are you going?"

"To stomp on their equipment! Jesus! What've we done?"

"Don't!" She seized his arm. "You'd just make trouble. After they've listened a few days they'll know we're okay and go away."

"I'm insulted, no, outraged! Those two words I've never used before, but, hell, they fit the case! Who do they think they are? Is it our politics? Our studio friends, my stories, the fact I'm a producer? Is it Tom Lee, because he's Chinese and a friend? Does that make him dangerous, or us? What, what?!"

"Maybe someone gave them a false lead and they're searching. If they really think we're dangerous, you can't blame them."

"I know, I know, but us! It's so damned funny I could laugh. Do we tell our friends? Rip out the microphone if we can find it, go to a hotel, leave town?"

"No, no, just go on as we have done. We've nothing to hide, so let's ignore them."

"Ignore!? The first thing I said tonight was political crap and you shut me up like I'd set off a bomb."

"Let's go in, it's cold out here. Be good. It'll only be a few days and they'll be gone, and after all, it isn't as if we were guilty of something."

"Yeah, okay, but damn, I wish you'd let me go over and kick the hell out of their junk!"

They hesitated, then entered the house, the strange house,

and stood for a moment in the hall trying to manufacture some appropriate dialogue. They felt like two amateurs in a shoddy out-of-town play, the electrician having suddenly turned on too much light, the audience, bored, having left the theater, and, simultaneously, the actors having forgotten their lines. So they said nothing.

He sat in the parlor trying to read the paper until the food was on the table. But the house suddenly echoed. The slightest crackle of the sports section, the exhalation of smoke from his pipe, became like the sound of an immense forest fire or a wind blowing through an organ. When he shifted in the chair the chair groaned like a sleeping dog, his tweed pants scraped and sandpapered together. From the kitchen there was an ungodly racket of pans being bashed, tins falling, oven doors cracking open, crashing shut, the fluming full-bloomed sound of gas jumping to life, lighting up blue and hissing under the inert foods, and then when the foods stirred ceaselessly under the commands of boiling water, they made a sound of washing and humming and murmuring that was excessively loud. No one spoke. His wife came and stood in the door for a moment, peering at her husband and the raw walls, but said nothing. He turned a page of football to a page of wrestling and read between the lines, scanning the empty whiteness and the specks of undigested pulp.

Now there was a great pounding in the room, like surf, growing nearer in a storm, a tidal wave, crashing on rocks and breaking with a titanic explosion again and again, in his ears.

My God, he thought, I hope they don't hear my heart!

His wife beckoned from the dining room, where, as he loudly rattled the paper and plopped it into the chair and walked, padding, padding on the rug, and drew out the protesting chair on the uncarpeted dining-room floor, she tinkled and clattered last-minute silverware, fetched a soup that bubbled like lava, and set a coffeepot to percolate beside them. They looked at the percolating silver apparatus, listened to it gargle in its glass throat, admired it for its protest against silence, for saying what it felt. And then there was the scrape and click of the knife and fork on the plate. He started to say something, but it stuck, with a morsel of food, in his throat. His eyes bulged. His wife's eyes bulged. Finally she got up, went to the kitchen, and got a piece of paper and a pencil. She came back and handed him a freshly written note: *Say something!*

He scribbled a reply:

What?

She wrote again: *Anything! Break the silence. They'll think something's wrong!*

They sat staring nervously at their own notes. Then, with a smile, he sat back in his chair and winked at her. She frowned. Then he said, "Well, dammit, say something!"

"What?" she said.

"Dammit," he said. "You've been silent all during supper. You and your moods. Because I won't buy you that coat, I suppose? Well, you're not going to get it, and that's final!"

"But I don't want—"

He stopped her before she could continue. "Shut up! I

won't talk to a nag. You know we can't afford mink! If you can't talk sense, don't talk!"

She blinked at him for a moment, and then she smiled and winked this time.

"I haven't got a thing to wear!" she cried.

"Oh, shut up!" he roared.

"You never buy me anything!" she cried.

"Blather, blather, blather!" he yelled.

They fell silent and listened to the house. The echoes of their yelling had put everything back to normalcy, it seemed. The percolator was not so loud, the clash of cutlery was softened. They sighed.

"Look," he said at last, "don't speak to me again this evening. Will you do me that favor."

She sniffed.

"Pour me some coffee!" he said.

Along about eight-thirty the silence was getting unbearable again. They sat stiffly in the living room, she with her latest library book, he with some flies he was tying up in preparation for going fishing on Sunday. Several times they glanced up and opened their mouths but shut them again and looked about as if a mother-in-law had hove into view.

At five minutes to nine he said, "Let's go to a show."

"This late?"

"Sure, why not?"

"You never like to go out weeknights, because you're tired. I've been home all day, cleaning, and it's nice to get out at night."

"Come on, then!"

"I thought you were mad at me."

"Promise not to talk mink and it's a go. Get your coat."

"All right." She was back in an instant, dressed, smiling, and they were out of the house and driving away in very little time. They looked back at their lighted house.

"Hail and farewell, house," he said. "Let's just drive and never come back."

"We don't dare."

"Let's sleep tonight in one of those motels that ruin your reputation," he suggested.

"Stop it. We've got to go back. If we stayed away, they'd be suspicious."

"Damn them. I feel like a fool in my own house. Them and their cricket."

"Bug."

"Cricket, anyway. I remember when I was a boy a cricket got in our house somehow. He'd be quiet most of the time, but in the evening he'd start scratching his legs together, an ungodly racket. We tried to find him. Never could. He was in a crack of the floor or the chimney somewhere. Kept us awake the first few nights, then we got used to him. He was around for half a year, I think. Then one night we went to bed and someone said, 'What's that noise?' and we all sat up, listening. 'I know what it is,' said Dad. 'It's silence. The cricket's gone.' And he was gone. Dead or went away, we never knew which. And we felt sort of sad and lonely with that new sound in the house."

They drove on the night road.

"We've got to decide what to do," she said.

"Rent a new house somewhere."

"We can't do that."

"Go to Ensenada for the weekend, we've been wanting to make that trip for years, do us good, they won't follow us and wire our hotel room, anyway."

"The problem'd still be here when we come back. No, the only solution is to live our life the way we used to an hour before we found out what was going on with the microphone."

"I don't remember. It was such a nice little routine. I don't remember how it was, the details, I mean. We've been married ten years now and one night's just like another, very pleasant, of course. I come home, we have supper, we read or listen to the radio, no television, and go to bed."

"Sounds rather drab when you say it like that."

"Has it been for you?" he asked suddenly.

She took his arm. "Not really. I'd like to get out more, occasionally."

"We'll see what we can do about that. Right now, we'll plan on talking straight out about everything, when we get back to the house, politically, socially, morally. We've nothing to hide. I was a Boy Scout when I was a kid, you were a Camp Fire Girl; that's not very subversive, it's as simple as that. Speak up. Here's the theater."

They parked and went into the show.

ABOUT MIDNIGHT THEY drove into the driveway of their house and sat for a moment looking at the great empty stage waiting for them. At last he stirred and said, "Well, let's go in and say hello to the cricket."

They garaged the car and walked around to the front door, arm in arm. They opened the front door and the feel of the atmosphere rushing out upon them was a listening atmosphere. It was like walking into an auditorium of one thousand invisible people, all holding their breath.

"Here we are!" said the husband loudly.

"Yes, that was a wonderful show, wasn't it?" said his wife.

It had been a pitiable movie.

"I liked the music especially!"

They had found the music banal and repetitive.

"Yes, isn't that girl a terrific dancer!"

They smiled at the walls. The girl had been a rather club-footed thirteen-year-old with an immensely low IQ.

"Darling!" he said. "Let's go to San Diego Sunday, for just the afternoon."

"What? And give up your fishing with your pals? You always go fishing with your pals." she cried.

"I won't go fishing with them this time. I love only you!" he said, and thought, miserably, We sound like Gallagher and Sheen warming up a cold house.

They bustled about the house, emptying ashtrays, getting ready for bed, opening closets, slamming doors. He sang a few bars from the tired musical they had seen in a lilting off-key baritone, she joining in.

In bed, with the lights out, she snuggled over against him, her hand on his arm, and they kissed a few times. Then they kissed a few more times. "This is more like it," he said. He gave her a rather long kiss. They snuggled even closer and he ran his hand along her back. Suddenly her spine stiffened.

Jesus, he thought, what's wrong now.

She pressed her mouth to his ear.

"What if," she whispered, "what if the cricket's in our bedroom, here?"

"They wouldn't dare!" he cried.

"Shh!" she said.

"They wouldn't dare," he whispered angrily. "Of all the nerve!"

She was moving away from him. He tried to hold her, but she moved firmly away and turned her back. "It would be just like them," he heard her whisper. And there he was, stranded on the white cold beach with the tide going out.

Cricket, he thought, I'll never forgive you for this.

The next day being Tuesday, he rushed off to the studio, had a busy day, and returned, on time, flinging open the front door with a cheery "Hey there, lovely!"

When his wife appeared, he kissed her solidly, patted her rump, ran an appreciative hand up and down her body, kissed her again, and handed her a huge green parcel of pink carnations.

"For me?" she said.

"You!" he replied.

"Is it our anniversary?"

"Nonsense, no. I just got them because, that's all, because."

"Why, how nice." Tears came to her eyes. "You haven't brought me flowers for months and months."

"Haven't I? I guess I haven't!"

"I love you," she said.

"I love you," he said, and kissed her again. They went, holding hands, into the living room.

"You're early," she said. "You usually stop off for a quick one with the boys."

"To hell with the boys. You know where we're going Saturday, darling? Instead of my sleeping in the backyard on the lounge, we're going to that fashion show you wanted me to go see."

"I thought you hated—"

"Anything you want, peaches," he said. "I told the boys I won't make it Sunday for the fishing trip. They thought I was crazy. What's for supper?"

He stalked smiling to the kitchen, where he appreciatively ladled and spooned and stirred things, smelling, gasping, tasting everything. "Shepherd's pie!" he cried, opening the oven and peering in, gloriously. "My God! My favorite dish. It's been since last June we had that!"

"I thought you'd like it!"

He ate with relish, he told jokes, they ate by candlelight, the pink carnations filled the immediate vicinity with a cinnamon scent, the food was splendid, and, topping it off, there was black-bottom pie fresh from the refrigerator.

"Black-bottom pie! It takes hours and genius to make a really good black-bottom pie."

"I'm glad you like it, dear."

After dinner he helped her with the dishes. Then they sat

on the living-room floor and played a number of favorite symphonies together, they even waltzed a bit to the *Rosenkavalier* pieces. He kissed her at the end of the dance and whispered in her ear, patting her behind, "Tonight, so help me God, cricket or no cricket."

The music started over. They swayed together.

"Have you found it yet?" he whispered.

"I think so. It's near the fireplace and the window."

They walked over to the fireplace. The music was very loud as he bent and shifted a drape, and there it was, a beady black little eye, not much bigger than a thumbnail. They both stared at it and backed away. He went and opened a bottle of champagne and they had a nice drink.

The music was loud in their heads, in their bones, in the walls of the house. He danced with his mouth up close to her ear.

"What did you find out?" she asked.

"The studio said to sit tight. Those damn fools are after everyone. They'll be tapping the zoo telephone next."

"Everything's all right?"

"Just sit tight, the studio said. Don't break any equipment, they said. You can be sued for breaking government property."

They went to bed early, smiling at each other.

On Wednesday night he brought roses and kissed her a full minute at the front door. They called up some brilliant and witty friends and had them over for an evening's discussion, having decided, in going over their phone list, that these two friends would stun the cricket with their repertoire and make the very air shimmer with their brilliance. On Thursday afternoon he called her from the studio for the first time in months, and on Thursday night he brought her an orchid, some more roses, a scarf he had seen in a shop window at lunchtime, and two tickets for a fine play. She in turn had baked him a chocolate cake from his mother's recipe, on Wednesday, and on Thursday had made Toll House cookies and lemon chiffon pie, as well as darning his socks and pressing his pants and sending everything to the cleaners that had been neglected previous times. They rambled about the town Thursday night after the play, came home late, read Euripides to one another out loud, went to bed late, smiling again, and got up late, having to call the studio and claim sickness until noon, when the husband, tiredly, on the way out of the house, thought to himself, This can't go on. He turned and came back in. He walked over to the cricket near the fireplace and bent down to it and said:

"Testing, one, two, three. Testing. Can you hear me? Testing."

"What're you doing?" cried his wife in the doorway.

"Calling all cars, calling all cars," said the husband, lines under his eyes, face pale. "This is me speaking. We know you're there, friends. Go away. Go away. Take your microphone and get out. You won't hear anything from us. That is all. That is all. Give my regards to J. Edgar. Signing off."

His wife was standing with a white and aghast look in the door as he marched by her, nodding, and thumped out the door.

She phoned him at three o'clock.

"Darling," she said, "it's gone!"

"The cricket?"

"Yes, they came and took it away. A man rapped very politely at the door and I let him in and in a minute he had unscrewed the cricket and taken it with him. He just walked off and didn't say boo."

"Thank God," said the husband. "Oh, thank God."

"He tipped his hat at me and said thanks."

"Awfully decent of him. See you later," said the husband.

This was Friday. He came home that night about six-thirty, having stopped off to have a quick one with the boys. He came in the front door reading his newspaper, passed his wife, taking off his coat and automatically putting it in the closet, went on past the kitchen without twitching his nose, sat in the living room and read the sports page until supper, when she served him plain roast beef and string beans, with apple juice to start and sliced oranges for dessert. On his way home he had turned in the theater tickets for tonight and tomorrow, he informed her; she could go with the girls to the fashion show, he intended to bake in the backyard.

"Well," he said, about ten o'clock. "The old house seems different tonight, doesn't it?"

"Yes."

"Good to have the cricket gone. Really had us going there."

"Yes," she said.

They sat awhile. "You know," she said later, "I sort of miss it, though, I really sort of miss it. I think I'll do something subversive so they'll put it back."

"I beg your pardon?" he said, twisting a piece of twine around a fly he was preparing from his fishing box.

"Never mind," she said. "Let's go to bed."

She went on ahead. Ten minutes later, yawning, he followed after her, putting out the lights. Her eyes were closed as he undressed in the semi-moonlit darkness. She's already asleep, he thought.

Afterword: Metaphors, the Breakfast of Champions

EVERY YEAR IN Paris, coming from the airport I have my driver pause at the Trocadero, a vast esplanade that overlooks the entire city with a splendid view of the Eiffel Tower.

I run out on this plaza, spread my arms, and cry, silently, "Paris, I'm home!"

When I leave, weeks later, I return to the plaza and, somewhat tearfully, say, "Paris, goodbye."

A few years ago when I crossed that twilight esplanade, it was raining.

My driver ran, shielding me with his umbrella. I fended him off with: "You don't understand, I *want* to get wet!"

So it is with these stories. Late in life I find I have been running a gauntlet downpour of metaphors. People try to shield me from this surprising storm, but my cry continues: "Don't! I *want* to drown!"

So, I've never worked a single hour in my life. For years metaphors bombarded me, but I never knew what they were, never having learned the word.

The recognition of metaphors came late when I found that ninety-nine percent of my stories were pure image, impacted by movies, the Sunday funnies, poetry, essays, and the detonations of Oz, Tarzan, Jules Verne, Pharaoh Tutankhamen, and their attendant illustrations.

In scanning this book I again realize how fortunate I was to live catching metaphors on the run.

The old question is repeated: Where do you get your ideas? Or rather, How do ideas run you down?

Many years ago I was successful in starting a film society for screenwriters. One of the first films we screened was the avant-garde *Last Year at Marienbad*, a somewhat bewildering production. During the viewing of the film the projectionist somehow reversed the reels and ran reel number ten after reel number five. No one noticed. Some in the audience even claimed that the picture was better than when first seen two weeks before! Need I say that I ran to my typewriter within hours to write the splendid film mix-up of "The Dragon Danced at Midnight?"

"Quid Pro Quo" is an almost true story. Forty years after my first encounter with a handsome young writer of immense talent, he shambled into my life, a derelict madman, empty of talent, lost to his promise and dreams. I was so brutalized by his self-destruction that "Quid Pro Quo" poured from my fingertips within hours.

A while back, I wrote a poem titled "I Am the Residue of

All My Daughters' Lives," touching on the fact that all of their past boyfriends, lovers, and fiancés stayed in touch with me long after being abandoned. I wrote "Leftovers" to fit the poem.

"The Nineteenth" is one more love offering to my father, who retired to play golf five days a week. One twilight I encountered him by the side of a golf-course path with a bucket, retrieving lost golf balls. The scene haunted me for years. My dad's fine ghost returned last year and I had to put him to rest.

In 1946 I often rode the Venice trolley Saturday midnights when the celebrants from Myron's Ballroom climbed on the streetcar to ride toward the sea. They were old white-haired men and women in tuxes and evening gowns. Some stepped off the trolley alone. Some strolled off into the dark in couples. Fifty-five years later, grown somewhat old and white myself, I had to step off the trolley to discover the rest of one couple's night journey with "After the Ball."

In high school, when copies of the neo-Renaissance magazine *Coronet* fell into my hands (I couldn't afford to buy it), I tore out photographs by Stieglitz, Karsh, and others and wrote poems to them. I didn't name what I did, just collected to worship pure image.

Lon Chaney dominated my life at three with *The Hunchback of Notre Dame.* Viewing it again when I was seventeen, I told friends I recalled the entire film. My friends scoffed. Okay, I said, there's this scene and that scene and this scene. Go see. We went, we saw. All the scenes were there as I remembered from my third year.

Much the same happened with *Phantom of the Opera* and

The Lost World. Chaney's Phantom and Willis O'Brien's dinosaurs haunted my childhood.

Chaney died in my tenth year and Death as a symbol fell into his grave. When his Phantom was re-released that year, I attended in agony, thinking that an abdominal pain was appendicitis. Weeping, I had to see the film even if I died. I lived, to dine on Chaney's metaphors for the rest of my life.

Some years later I formed a lifelong friendship with Ray Harryhausen, who ran dinosaur metaphors in his garage to become the greatest stop-motion animator of our age. My God, the persistence of metaphor in our incredible friendship!

Laurel and Hardy have shaped three of my fictions. I arrived in Dublin in October 1953, and there in the *Irish Times* saw this:

Today Only
In Person
Olympia Theatre
Laurel and Hardy

"My God," I cried, "we've got to go!"

My wife said, "Go!"

One ticket remained, front row, center.

I sat, tears streaming, as Stan and Ollie performed scenes from all the years of my life.

Outside their dressing-room door I watched Stan and Ollie greet friends. I didn't intrude, relishing their ambience, then went away.

Their ghosts went with me. I wrote two stories about Stan and Ollie. And, now, a third for this book.

In other words, once a metaphor, always a metaphor.

I learned more of my inner self from film director Sam Peckinpah, who loved to pour vodka in my beer. He wanted to film my novels.

"Sam," I said, "how will you *do* it?"

"Rip the pages out of your books," Sam said, "and stuff them in the camera!"

So I found that by a lifetime of mad film attendance the mad paragraphs of my novels were close-ups and long shots.

With my *Ray Bradbury Theater* on television, I learned I could type my stories straight from the book into teleplays.

"Stuff your pages," echoed Sam, "in the camera!"

Thus I had digested cinema metaphors, in ignorant bliss, to deliver forth films.

Then again, simply put, I have never been jealous of other writers, only wanted to protect them. So many of my most beloved authors have suffered unhappy lives or incredibly unhappy endings. I had to invent machines to travel in time to protect them, or at least say *I love you*. Those machines are here.

And here, finally, is that downpour of images from photos, films, cartoons, encounters that have tracked through life without an umbrella.

How fortunate I've been to pace such storms and emerge wonderfully drenched and alive to finish this book.

Ray Bradbury
Los Angeles, April 2001